I0567715

JASPER LILLA
AND THE
FLIGHT TO BOONE

C.S. THOMPSON

Published in the U.S. by:
James One Institute
Bristol, TN

Csthompsonbooks.com

Copyright © 2016 by CS Thompson.

All right reserved.

ISBN: 978-0-99046-013-8

This is a work of fiction. Names, characters, events, and incidents are either the products of the author's imagination or are used in a fictitious manner.

Although the major characters are all fictional and any resemblance to a real person is accidental and unintentional, many of the places and events are real and the people one would find there are real as well.

Cover design by CS Thompson & Cam Collins
  (www.camelliadigital.com)
Interior design by Gary A. Rosenberg
  (www.thebookcouple.com)

CONTENTS

PROLOGUE

IT WOKE HER AGAIN. It was happening much more frequently now. The sudden rush of being snatched from the ground and taken to a dizzying height pushed her stomach toward her feet and beyond. The suddenness of the lift was worse than the drop of any roller coaster. *Don't look,* she told herself every time it happened. But she would look. Hoping to discover it was only a dream, she'd open her eyes and look. What she'd see was always different, yet always the same, too. It was always the earth far below her, but it was always a different part of the earth. It looked to be miles below, and yet she could see it with the clarity of twenty feet. She could only keep her eyes open for a moment because the height was terrifying. She knew she couldn't survive a fall from where she was, but that isn't what scared her. From that height, the death flight would give her plenty of time to think as she fell. She was utterly and completely at the mercy of whoever or whatever snatched her from the earth. All she needed to do was look up to discover in whose control she was, but she could never gather the courage to look.

This time was unusual, though. This time she could feel its grasp on her arms—and then it shook her, not hard, but deliberately. She heard a voice.

"You're okay."

It was a man's voice. He was close, very close.

"You're okay."

I'm not, she thought, fighting the temptation to open her eyes.

"It's just a dream."

It isn't, she thought. *I'll fall.*

"You're okay."

She could feel him leaning against her. She could feel something supporting her back, her whole body. She recognized his voice. Her eyes opened enough to peek at him.

I am okay, she shuddered as she threw her arms around him, drawing him closer still. Holding on to him as if she might fall if she didn't, she began to sob.

He gently rubbed her back until her sobbing slowed. Then he asked, "Was it that same dream?"

"I don't know what that was," she said, "but it was no dream."

CHAPTER 1

FLIGHT TO BOONE

IT WAS MY JEEP CHEROKEE WAITING FOR ME at the curb when I exited the building. Evans and Harlan were already in the backseat. Maire was in the driver's seat, and next to her was Riley. There wasn't room for me in the front, but I slid in next to Riley and shut the door.

"Are you ready, Jasper?" asked Maire.

I didn't know how to answer the question right away. I was ready. Of course I was ready. I had been ready to take Riley home since the minute she was kidnapped from in front of Galileo's in Boone. It wasn't my fault she was kidnapped, but it was hard not to blame myself anyway. The kidnappers were probably trying to take me, and settled for her instead. And if that's not enough, the person behind the kidnapping turned out to be a sister I never knew I had.

Aayma, the unknown sister, was no ordinary person. Our mother, Vernalisa, is Mother Nature. I didn't know about Mom until just before Riley was taken. That didn't give me enough time to understand what having Mother Nature for my mom meant. Then, before leaving the building where we rescued Riley, I found out that our assailant was my sister, and she is no more ordinary

1

than our mother. So, was I ready? You bet I was, but more than that, I was dumbfounded.

I didn't have to answer Maire's question, though, because Aiden followed right after me, and as soon as I shut the door he leaned in to speak to Maire.

"Get them out of here before the police arrive," Aiden told Maire. Scanning his eyes across the rest of us he added, "We'd rather the Hendersonville Police not know you kids were here."

"But they know Riley was here," objected Harlan.

"Yes, and she'll have to come back to be questioned, but we can delay that for now," Aiden answered.

Riley nodded an acknowledgment that she'd have to be questioned at some point. "I just want to go home," she said, sounding exhausted.

"I know," Aiden said. "Maire will get you home." As he said that his head jerked back to his left. I could tell he had heard something.

It took a few moments for us to hear it, too. It was a siren. The police were on the way.

"Fly!" exclaimed Aiden, stepping back from the car.

And fly she did.

Maire drove like a maniac until we were out of Hendersonville and headed north on Route 26. Mostly we rode in silence until we were well past Asheville. Riley and I didn't last too long trying to sit crammed together in the passenger seat. She ended up on my lap with her head on my shoulder. My right arm was around her back and my right leg was throbbing. It had been asleep for a while. There was no way I was going to say anything. She was asleep before we hit I-40 West.

Evans and Harlan were quiet in the backseat, too, which I welcomed. I desperately wanted it all to be over, and having Riley next to me was supposed to mean that it was all over. I kept repeating in my mind, *Riley's home now.* But I feared it wasn't over. I wanted to feel safe and normal, whatever normal is.

I knew Aayma had been behind it all from the beginning, and she had escaped. "From the beginning" was an interesting phrase for me to use because I had no idea where the beginning was. Aayma had come after me when I was ten. She had come after my father when I was a baby. She was my mother's daughter. That thought made me shudder enough to unsettle Riley.

Riley looked at me through half-opened eyes.

"I'm okay," I murmured. "Go back to sleep."

She did, and I reluctantly went back to my thoughts.

My mother's words—"Aayma is disease"—began to swim around in my head. Luckily my vibrating phone brought me out of that depth before my head exploded.

I looked at my phone. It showed a text from Mr. Gabriel, my school counselor: "Come see me Friday morning during second period."

We were still a half hour south of Boone when Maire huffed and pulled into the parking lot of an abandoned restaurant.

"What's the matter?" asked Harlan.

"It's the police," said Maire. "I might have been going a little fast."

"You were flying," said Evans.

"Let's hope that's all it is," said Maire, just as there came a tap on the window.

Maire lowered her window, and Detective Nora Charles from Boone leaned in.

"Hello, Riley," she said.

"Hello," said Riley weakly. She had woken up a bit when the car stopped, but she wasn't entirely awake.

"We haven't met," continued Detective Charles, "but I'm the officer assigned to your case. We're all very glad to see you come home."

"Is she in there?" shouted a man from the car behind us.

Nora grinned. "That's your father, Riley. He's pretty anxious to get you home. I was with him when I got the call that you were on your way home. He couldn't wait."

"Daddy," said Riley, still weak, but stronger and more awake than her greeting to the detective. She strained to look back but didn't see him because he had circled around to my side of the car.

"Baby!" exclaimed Riley's dad, King Lyons, as he tried to open my door.

Riley and I had to shift around a bit so that when I unlocked the door we wouldn't immediately fall out. As it was, I barely made it out of the way before Riley's dad swept her up and began to cry loudly.

"I'm okay, I'm okay," Riley told him.

We all just waited awkwardly, because it didn't feel right to watch, but there was nothing else to do either. Finally Detective Charles put her hand on King's back and said, "We've got to get her to the doctor's office."

King nodded and began leading Riley back to the police car behind us.

Detective Charles stepped closer to the open door where I sat half in and half out. "We're just going to get her checked out by her doc. I'm sure you'll see her back at school in a day or two."

A day or two? I thought I was going to cry. Watching her walk away didn't help either. Then she stopped walking and said something to her dad. He looked at her, and then he looked at me and nodded.

Riley walked slowly back toward me holding her arms around her middle, like she was cold, but it wasn't cold. I wasn't sure what was going to happen, but I knew I needed to stand up and walk toward her.

When she got close enough she put her arms around my middle and said, "Thank you." Then she kissed me. It wasn't a long kiss, but it wasn't a kiss on the cheek either. I was so surprised she kissed me on the mouth in front of her dad that I don't know if I even kissed her back. I do know her kiss was salty.

CHAPTER 2

HOME

DISAPPOINTMENT WAS THE LEAST OF WHAT I FELT as we drove the last leg of our flight to Boone. There was so much I wanted to say to Riley that I was unsure of what any of it was, but I knew there was a lot of it. Maybe there was just a lot I wanted to hear from her—and now I'd have to wait again. That's what was on my mind when Maire and I walked into our kitchen.

My older sister Carol and her husband, Wally, were sitting at the table, and Aunt Maggie was in her usual spot by the stove, although we were well past dinnertime.

As soon as we walked in, Aunt Maggie said, "Kitty needs to get out to the back pasture."

"I'll do it," volunteered Maire right away. She patted her thigh and Kitty, our 110-pound Great Pyrenees dog, followed her out the back door. Nothing would disturb our alpaca through the night. Kitty would see to that.

"The school called," Carol said coolly.

The thought that someone from the school called alarmed me. I didn't care so much if I got caught, and I doubted if Harlan or Evans would care either. But Cathy had covered for us in the attendance office while we went to Hendersonville, so it would be a big deal if she got caught.

"What did they want?" I asked.

"It was a Mr. Gabor," said Maggie.

"Gabriel," I suggested.

"Yes," Maggie said. "That's it, Mr. Gabriel."

"He said he was concerned since you missed two days and then didn't return his text," said Carol, sipping her tea while eyeing me over the edge of the cup.

I had completely forgotten about his text, but I remembered it when she mentioned it. "I have a meeting with him Monday morning," I told her. "He rent a seminder." I shrugged, "I didn't know I needed to respond."

"Are you nervous?" asked Carol.

"No, not at all," I said as boldly as I could. I wondered what I had done to alert her.

"You said, 'He rent a seminder,'" she told me. "You usually do that when you're nervous."

I smiled at her as best I could.

In an exaggerated innocent voice Carol asked, "Jasper, have you missed two days of school?"

"His absences were excused," said Maire before I could answer. I hadn't heard her come back in. "He helped Aiden and me in the investigation of the abduction of Riley Lyons."

"Really?" said Carol.

"Yes," said Maire. "And I am pleased to announce that Aiden was able to recover Miss Lyons this afternoon."

"Riley's back," blurted Wally. "I'll bet King is ecstatic." He held up his hand for a high five.

"He is," I said, completing the high five.

"I'm guessing you're ecstatic, too, aren't you?" asked Carol. She had set her cup down and hugged me. Her tone was completely different.

As I hugged her I looked at Maire and mouthed, "Thank you."

Maggie saw, but didn't react. Neither did Maire.

"So," continued Carol, when she let me go, "how did you fit into the equation?"

"We took Jazz-barr because of his familiarity with the victim. He was of great comfort to her once she was recovered," Maire told them, just before answering her phone. "Excuse me," she said, heading out the back door again.

"Soup?" offered Maggie with a bowl of what looked like her corn chowder in her hand. She pointed at my spot at the table, and I obeyed.

I sat down and was about halfway finished with the soup when Maire returned.

"That was Aiden," she told us. "He says he and Vernalisa are still in Hendersonville. They aren't suspects, but they are required to stay in town for a while because of the murders of James Benjamin and Detective Ward."

I had been there in the room when both of those men were murdered. Neither Mom nor Aiden were there, but they were there when the police arrived, so of course they had to answer questions. I couldn't imagine what they were telling the police.

"We need a favor," began Carol. "Actually, it's just as much for you as it is for us."

"What?" I asked.

She grinned, "As you know, Dr. Lyons has been selling off his business."

I nodded yes.

"Well," her smile got bigger, "he closed the final part of the deal yesterday, and it didn't include the research lab." She bobbed her head slightly, trying to coax me into finishing her sentence.

"If you're okay with it, he's giving the lab to you and Wally." She gently slapped my shoulder. "What do you think of that?"

I'm sure my reaction didn't meet her expectation. Normal

juniors in high school would be a bit excited to hear that they had just inherited a research lab. But all I could think about was what would happen to Riley. If her dad sold his whole business, what would keep them in Boone?

CHAPTER 3

MR. GABRIEL

I'M NOT SURE HOW I MANAGED TO GET TO SLEEP, but finally I did. I don't think it was a very good sleep because when I got out of bed the next morning my covers were in a knot and off the end of the bed. I also hadn't planned on getting up and going to school, but Aunt Maggie didn't give me an option.

"I can help out here," I said at the breakfast table.

Maggie shook her head no. "There is nothing for you to do."

"I can help out in the lab," I said.

Carol responded to that ploy. "Wally said he'd just be doing inventory and packing today. Besides, you have that appointment with your school counselor."

"Is it safe?" I asked with my last attempt.

"It is safe," Maggie answered. "When Aayma comes again, it will be at night."

Carol and I looked at each other. I suppose Carol wanted to see if I knew what Maggie was talking about. I didn't. My look at Carol was to see if she'd ask the question.

"Why at night?" asked Carol.

"She knows we know she is here, so she can no longer surprise us," began Maggie.

I doubt that, I thought, and I'm certain Carol doubted it, too.

"She cannot transform her servants during the day, not like the Mother can."

"Do you mean she can make them human?" asked Carol.

"She can," answered Maggie, "but only at night. And she cannot give them the power to transform themselves."

"Like you can," I observed.

"Yes," said Maggie.

"What's it like?" asked Carol.

"It is something that feels very natural to me, but I have been serving your mother my whole life, as did my mother before me, and her mother before her. But I can tell you what Aiden has told me."

"He's a wolf," I told Carol, not sure if she remembered. She nodded that she did.

"Aiden and his pack are Russian wolves. They were fully grown when the Mother brought them here. According to Aiden, learning to move from a pure state to a human state is like learning a new language. Until it became natural to him, he had problems remembering what to do as a human; at first, he kept thinking and acting like a wolf, having to tell himself to wear clothes and walk upright. But now that he is used to it, when he is human he thinks and acts human." She rolled her hand over. "Do you see?"

"Yes," answered Carol.

"Good," said Maggie. "Now, no more questions." Pointing at me she ordered, "Go to school."

❧

Second period came, and I was excused from my world history class to go to Mr. Gabriel's office. He arrived at his door at the same time as I did.

"Good morning, Jasper," said Mr. Gabriel, opening the door.

"Good morning," I returned.

I sat in the upholstered chair across from his desk as he hung his sports coat on a hook on the back of his door.

Sitting in the chair next to me, he patted my forearm and said, "I had a nice conversation with Miss Lyons this morning. She tells me you're quite the hero."

I didn't know what to say. I didn't know how much he knew about last week, but it was a good bet he knew I wasn't at home sick.

"Relax," he told me. "I'm not the truancy officer."

I assumed that meant he wasn't going to tell anyone what we had done.

"How was she?" I asked.

He smiled. "All things considered, she is doing incredibly well. Her doctor checked her out and gave her a clean bill of health. She has an acute stress reaction, but that's to be expected with everything she's been through. She's lost fifteen pounds, and she was sleep deprived. The doctor prescribed rest and suggested she talk to a counselor. That's why her dad called me."

"Are you going to be her counselor?" I asked.

"No, but I gave her dad a couple of names of folks in town. She got an appointment with someone this afternoon." He leaned toward me. "She asked me to tell you that she hasn't contacted you because she doesn't have a new phone yet." Raising an eyebrow he added, "I don't think she's going to get a new one unless the counselor okays it either."

It scared me that she was being sent to a counselor. "Is she going to be okay?"

"I think so," he said, looking more seriously. "She said you'd question me and she told me that I could tell you whatever you asked. So to answer your question more fully, yes, she's going to be okay, but she may not be okay right away. There's no evidence that she was tortured or violated in any way other than the trauma of being abducted and held captive for a couple of weeks. But how threatened she was is a little harder to tell. When people go through what she went through, their memories often get out of whack. That's what the counselor will help her straighten out." His gaze drifted away from me for a moment. "There is one minor concern. She says the men who took her were birds."

"Birds!" I repeated.

"Yes," he said. "Buzzards. But I'm not too worried about that, and you shouldn't worry about that either, Jasper."

You have no idea, I thought.

"A brief period of hallucinations is quite common with prolonged sleep deprivation. That's what I told Mr. Lyons, too. He seemed quite alarmed, but I reassured him that there's no reason to be overly concerned because she saw buzzards. A few good nights of sleep will take care of that."

I wondered.

"If we've covered Riley sufficiently, can we talk about the reason I asked you here this morning?" asked Mr. Gabriel, adding, "I'm sure you're wondering about that yourself."

"I am," I admitted.

"It's your junior year. If you're going to college after high school you'll need to start applying next year, and if you're going to do that, then you need to start thinking about your future now. Have you started thinking about your future, Jasper?"

"No. I mean, yes. I mean, sort of," I said. I didn't know what I was saying.

Mr. Gabriel chuckled. "You'd be surprised at how often I get just exactly that answer. Tell me, if you had to pick a vocation right now, what would it be?"

"Do you mean a job? What job would I pick?"

"A vocation is bigger than that, but that's a good place to start. What job would you pick if you could pick?"

It felt like we were playing a game I didn't want to play. My future job was not on my list of concerns. On the other hand, there didn't seem to be a way out of the conversation. *Do what you have to do to get this over with,* was the advice I gave myself.

"I've been helping my brother-in-law in his lab," I said. "That seems like something I could do."

"There you go," he said. "What have you been doing?"

"He runs the research lab out at Lion Pharmaceuticals, and I've been helping identify what antidotes go with what poison."

"Really?" He sounded like he didn't believe me. He reached for a file on his desk and opened it. "I don't mean to sound rude, Jasper, but that kind of work just surprised me is all."

It made me a little mad that he didn't believe that I could do something important.

Looking up from the file he said, "Your academic record is very confusing, Jasper, but now that I look at it again, I really shouldn't be surprised at anything you do."

This made me even angrier.

He looked at me and saw something on my face. "Oh, Jasper, please. I fear I have insulted you. Please believe me, that is not my intention. It's just that you've taken the bare minimum science classes." He closed the file. "Usually people who want to do research take science classes, especially science classes with labs. You lean toward literature classes."

"My mother's an author," I told him.

"Yes. Vernalisa Vanderguard. She's very good. And undoubtedly she has instilled in you a love for the spoken word," he responded. "Passion will outweigh skills every time." As soon as he said that, he looked surprised. "I hope that didn't insult you again, Jasper, but I know you have trouble with some dyslexia, too."

"That's okay," I told him, but truthfully it hadn't dawned on me to be insulted by his comment. "As far as I know," I confessed, "I've only got one skill."

"I very much doubt that," he said. "But it's nice that you are clear about one skill. What is it?"

"I smell," I told him.

"I'm not sure that's a skill you can get paid for," he said. He was serious.

I knew I had said it in a confusing way, but since I was yet to explain it well, I decided to amuse myself with how I said it. This was my first attempt at amusement.

"Dr. Beery, the researcher, says I have enhanced olfactory sensitivity," I explained.

"You smell," repeated Mr. Gabriel with a nod and a smile.

I nodded.

"It's a gift," he said.

"It's a gift?" I questioned.

"A gift," he explained. "It's like a skill, but you didn't manufacture it so much as you discovered it, and after you discover it you keep developing it." He looked deeper into my eyes. "You were born with it, right?"

I nodded yes.

"So let me ask you this: Are you passionate about your work in the lab?"

I had to think about the question. In the beginning it was just something I could do. Then, when we found out I was good at it, it made me feel good about myself. It made me think I could actually deserve to be with Riley. Then Riley was taken, and it was all because disease didn't want me to find cures, and that's where I got stuck.

"I can see you're thinking about it," observed Mr. Gabriel.

I looked at him and wondered for a moment if he could read

my mind. He was right. I was thinking about it. I didn't want to put Riley at risk again, but the thought of letting Aayma win made me mad.

"I'm going to let you head on to third period, Jasper, but I'd like to see you next week. Is that okay?"

"Yeah," I agreed.

"Great, Jasper. You see, this is much more about you being true to the real you than it is about getting you to the right college major or vocation. It might be a bit corny to say, but the truth is, you only have two choices here: You can be you, or less."

I knew what he just said was important to him, so to humor him I asked, "Can I ask a quick question first?"

"Of course," he said as he stood.

I stood up, too. "How do you know what you should do?"

He laughed and patted me on the shoulder. "That, my friend, was not a quick question, but here's the quick answer. Knowing what you should do is what we've been talking about, and it will be what we talk about every time we meet. Does that clear it up?"

"A little," I said, but I didn't mean it.

CHAPTER 4

A NOT-SO-FRIENDLY WARNING

THE REST OF THE SCHOOL DAY WAS TORTUROUS. My time with Mr. Gabriel was the only time all day that I could slow my mind down. My mind was like a Ping-Pong ball bouncing back and forth between thoughts of Riley and thoughts of Aayma. With the exception of Mr. Gabriel I couldn't remember anything about the day when I drove home. Anticipating seeing my mother at home had the effect of keeping the Ping-Pong ball on Aayma's side of the net.

I had been thinking of questions for my mother about Aayma for over twenty-four hours, so that's what was in my mind when I drove up the driveway to our home. What I saw when I turned the corner to the back of the house was a conclave between Carol, Maggie, Maire, and Wally. I hit the brakes, because whatever they were talking about was serious, and I was well past my capacity for serious.

Carol saw me and waved me over to my usual parking place. By the time I had backed into my spot, Carol was standing next to my window.

"We need your friends," she said as I opened the door.

Ignoring her, I asked, "Where's Mom?"

"She and Maire's husband are still hung up in Hendersonville.

They're still answering questions about the deaths of that man who killed Doctor Dietrich and the police detective who gave you a hard time were killed in the same apartment where they were holding Riley."

"They didn't have anything to do with that," I said immediately. I knew for sure they didn't have anything to do with it because I watched it happen.

"Of course they didn't," said Carol. "They aren't under arrest or anything. They just couldn't leave Hendersonville until now. They'll be here in a few hours."

"Rats!" I said.

"We need your friends," Carol said again. "Can you round up a few? We'll pay ten dollars an hour."

"For what?" I asked.

"Remember? Riley's dad sold his company the same day as you brought Riley back. He sold the patents to another pharmaceutical company. The Parks Department bought the building." She paused and smiled at me before saying, "And he gave the lab to you and Wally."

I remembered, but what all that meant didn't sink into me as much as Carol expected.

"Earth to Jasper," said Carol as she poked me in the ribs.

I tried to concentrate on her, but my heart was not in it.

"Before you drift off into another daydream, please call a few of your friends and get us some day labor. Tonight, we need to move my studio into storage until we can get the loft above the birthing barn ready. Then, tomorrow morning we'll move everything from the lab over at Lion to my studio. We've got to get it done tomorrow, so we'll need lots of help. Can you do it?"

"I'll call and ask," I told her.

"Thanks," she said. "Let me know when you're done."

I called Harlan first. She said she could and she was sure

Evans and Dirk were free. I called Evans next. He said he could help, and he'd get Dirk, too. He even said he was sure Dirk could get a truck for us also. It only took ten minutes to make those calls, but that was long enough for me to walk well into the forest preserve to the east of our house. I did not want anyone to hear my next phone call.

Forgetting Riley's message about not having a new phone yet, I dialed her old phone number. "Riley," I said excitedly when the ringing stopped.

"Hello, Jasper," replied a breathy woman's voice.

I stopped breathing.

"Were you expecting Riley?" she asked in a voice that made me nauseated.

I pulled the phone away from my ear as fast as I could and turned it off. I shuddered as I turned to head back to the Lilla compound. The next thing I knew I was dangling in the air. One of those vulture freaks had his hands around my neck and had lifted me off the ground.

"She wasn't finished talking to you yet," he said through clenched teeth. "Call again," he ordered as he dropped me to the ground.

From where I lay on the ground looking up I could see another three vultures perched in the trees above me. The only one in human form was the one who had manhandled me.

I made the call.

"This is a friendly warning, Jasper," she said. "Tell your family their time is over. It's my time now. Don't stand in my way."

"What do you mean?" I begged.

The phone went dead. I was too afraid to move until I watched as the vultures took flight one by one.

CHAPTER 5

SATURDAY MORNING

BY SATURDAY MORNING I COULDN'T REMEMBER anything about school on Friday. I remember talking to Mr. Gabriel. I remember arranging for Evans and Dirk to help me move the lab and for Harlan to help Carol and Maire at Carol's studio. And I remember Aayma telling me to get out of the way. I do remember what I didn't do; I didn't talk to Riley, and I didn't talk to Mom. In spite of the fact that it kept me up half the night, I decided not to tell anyone about that conversation until I talked to Mom first.

Harlan wasn't able to help, but since we couldn't get the truck to move the lab until after three o'clock, Carol and Maire had plenty of time to pack up and move her studio without Harlan. I went with Wally to run some errands around town, which I think was mostly to be out of Carol's way until three o'clock.

Wally had spent his Friday putting numbered stickers on all the boxes in the lab. Some of the warehouse guys had boxed everything up on Thursday. The wheelchair kept Wally from supervising both inside the lab and outside in the truck, so he put numbers on boxes. All we had to do was carry the boxes out in numerical order.

We had a flat cart and two dollies. We'd take boxes out to the curb where Dirk had parked the truck his father let us borrow. Wally, clipboard in hand, kept track of what was in each box so that we wouldn't stack heavy boxes on top of boxes of breakables. Whenever we had accumulated a dozen or so boxes on the curb Dirk would climb inside the truck while Evans and I lifted boxes up to him. Wally told Dirk how to stack them.

"You guys are great," encouraged Wally as we headed back in for the last few boxes. "Refreshments are on the way."

"Éclairs?" asked Evans, sounding like Kitty would sound if he were begging for bacon.

"I don't know, but I'm sure you won't be disappointed," Wally reassured him.

Once we were inside Dirk shoved Evans. "Do you have éclairs on the brain or something?"

Shoving Dirk back, Evans said, "I can't help it. You had one of those éclairs from that place in Hendersonville. You said it was the best, and I never got a chance to get one myself."

"Are you mental?" I blurted.

The question surprised everyone, even me. I had never joined in when they took shots at each other, so this was completely unexpected. When they took shots at each other they were being playful, but what had come out of my mouth was part shock and part anger.

"You didn't get an éclair because we saved Riley instead," I said.

"I know," sighed Evans. Then he stepped closer and put his hand on my shoulder. I was a little scared he would be mad that I yelled at him, but he wasn't. "I was there, wasn't I?"

I nodded yes.

"And if we had to do it all over again, I'd do it again," he boasted.

"I know, " I said. I was embarrassed.

As we headed back down the hall to the lab Evans said, "I still hope it's éclairs."

"Are you kidding me?" said Evans through clinched teeth. He was struggling to lift the crate labeled 61. Standing up and exhaling loudly he said, "I know why this is the last one. It has to be at the back of the truck."

Dirk strutted over to his friend. "Are you feeling okay?" He pointed at me with his thumb. "Would you like Jasper to take this one?

They both looked at me. I knew I was expected to add something clever to the banter, but it wasn't in me. They didn't wait long.

"Bring that cart closer," Dirk told me.

The cart he was referring to was a small four-wheeled flat that steered like a wagon. We had borrowed it from the warehouse. I got it as close to crate number 1 as I could, and the two of them wrestled it up on the cart while I held it steady.

We placed our last load at the curb but agreed to wait until after snack time to try and get that last crate up on the bed of the truck. I was pretty sure we were going to have to empty and repack whatever was in there.

"We're almost done, guys," said Wally. "Thanks. My friend Oberon is on the way." He looked at Evans. "It's not éclairs, I'm afraid. It's paninis."

"From Bombadil's?" asked Dirk.

"You know Bombadil's?" asked Wally.

The three of us just looked at each other. Finally I said, "We've been there once."

"So you've met Oberon," said Wally.

"We saw his table, but he wasn't there the night we were there," said Evans.

"How do you know Oberon?" I asked Wally.

Wally mimicked picking something up with his fingertips and

setting it back down in my direction. "Oberon and I play chess sometimes. I started going to his restaurant for lunch when work here slowed down, and since I was eating alone I played chess on my computer. Oberon asked me if I'd rather play something breathing, and we've been playing ever since."

"How is he?" asked Dirk.

Wally laughed to himself. "His biggest problem as a chess player is that his hands are so big he tends to knock other pieces over when he picks one up. I win occasionally, but he's definitely the superior player."

"Not true," came a deep voice from behind us. It sounded like someone talking in a barrel.

"Hello, Oberon," said Wally. I'm sure he knew the big man was right behind us and wanted to watch us react.

I don't know if Dirk or Evans did what I did, but Wally got a good show from me. After I flinched my shoulders up, I turned around looking for someone at my eye level and immediately had to throw my head back enough to nearly tip me over.

Oberon was a good head and shoulders taller than Evans. His hands and arms were massive, as was his belly. His baggy overalls hid his legs, but they had to be strong enough to hold up the top half of him. Between his hair and beard his round face was completely surrounded by bushy brown hair. He didn't smile when he looked at you, but he didn't look angry either. He just looked at you like he was waiting for you to do something.

Dirk was the first one to speak. "Hi, sir," he said extending his hand. "I sure enjoyed your restaurant the time I was there."

Dirk's hand disappeared in Oberon's, as the big man nodded yes. I have no idea how nodding yes was a response to what Dirk said, but I wasn't going to say anything.

"Me, too," said Evans, extending his hand. He received the same response as Dirk.

"I liked Zella," I told him, half expecting my hand to be crushed when he took hold of it. Zella was the hostess of Oberon's restaurant, Bombadil's.

"Me, too," said Oberon. His grip on my hand was barely noticeable.

Oberon stepped around us and put a large brown paper bag on Wally's lap. "Lunch," he declared.

"Thank you," said Wally. "I'm sure it will be wonderful."

Oberon nodded yes again and then walked over to the crate at the curb and placed it on the bed of the truck.

CHAPTER 6

BACK AT THE FARM

"DID YOU SEE THAT?" asked Dirk under his breath.

"I know. It's incredible," responded Evans with his mouth full. He thought Dirk was referring to the bag full of sandwiches. He had missed Oberon's display of strength because he was digging into his panini.

We made quick work of the sandwiches. Mine was cheese, tomato, and basil.

It was close to seven o'clock when we finished loading the truck and were ready to head back to the farm. Dirk and Evans had to take off, so I hoped the unloading would be a Sunday chore.

Oberon drove the truck back to the farm, and Wally drove his van, so it was my duty to drive Oberon's Jeep Wrangler for him. His Jeep was missing the roof and the sides, which made it fun to drive, but I kept picturing the oversized man sitting in it, head peaking over the windshield, the seat all the way back, and his body hanging out past where the door would have been.

As I followed up the long drive I couldn't see what was waiting for me in the open area between our house and the outbuildings behind it. The largest outbuilding was directly across from our kitchen door. That's where Carol and Wally lived, and that's also where Carol's studio was being converted to a research lab. To the right of Carol's house was an all-purpose barn. That's where we did the shearing every spring. Further to the right was another smaller barn. That was the birthing barn. It had an upstairs loft that we'd be converting into a studio for Carol. Our name for the entire collection of buildings was the Lilla Compound, or more often just "the compound." The middle of the compound was a wide-open space where we parked our cars. Mom had it blacktopped for Wally.

To my delight and joy, right there in the middle of our compound was my mother. She and Aiden must have just arrived from Hendersonville because the trunk of her car was still open and being attended by Aiden. Mom was standing with Maire and Carol. From the way her arms were gesturing, I'd guess that Carol was doing most of the talking.

As I parked Oberon's Jeep beside Carol's car I was thankful I didn't have to navigate that truck up our drive and around into this area backward. That's what Oberon had to do because there was nowhere to turn around if he came in frontward.

"When did you get home?" I asked Mom.

"Just a few minutes ago," she said, hugging me.

When Wally pulled into his parking spot Carol left us alone.

"We need to talk, Mom," I said under my breath.

"I know," she said under her breath. "Tonight."

"Does Carol know?"

"About Aayma?" Mom questioned back.

"Yeah. Does Carol know about her?"

"I don't think so. Did you say anything to her?" Mom asked me.

"I didn't, but I wouldn't know what to tell her anyway."

"We'll talk tonight, and then we'll talk to Carol. I promise," said Mom. She turned her head to watch Carol and Wally approaching.

26

As they continued past us Carol said, "I'm going to show Wally what I was thinking about the back side of the loft."

"Carol wants to put an outdoor set of stairs up to the loft so she won't disturb any of the girls in the birthing barn," Mom explained to me. Just before Carol and Wally turned the corner, Mom called out to them, "Be careful. It can be muddy back there."

"We're okay," returned Carol.

Watching them disappear, Mom said, "It's good she doesn't baby him in that wheelchair, but sometimes I think she doesn't account for it either."

It didn't seem like she was really talking to me, so I didn't say anything. Besides, that is when the back of the truck came into view. Oberon stopped the truck and came around to open the back end.

"Oh, my," said Mom. "Carol said he was big, but he is *big*." We walked toward the back of the truck.

Oberon saw us coming toward him and took a step in our direction.

"You must be Mr. Oberon," said Mom.

"It's 'Oberon,' Mom, not 'Mr. Oberon,'" Carol explained, coming up behind us.

"Hello," said Oberon, gently taking Mom's hand.

Still holding Oberon's hand, Mom said to Carol, "You weren't back there very long."

"Wally got a wheel stuck in the mud, thank you very much," said Carol. To Oberon she asked, "Do you think you could help him before he burns up the motor?"

Oberon nodded yes and began walking in the direction Carol came from.

"No! Get away!"

The scream was Wally, but it didn't sound like him. I recognized the panic in it, but I had never heard him sound like that before. My instinct was to stop where I was and look around for danger. I was the only one who did that, though. Mom, Carol, and Oberon each immediately began moving in the direction of the scream.

Oberon was ahead of us, so he was the first to turn the corner. Carol, screaming, "Wally! Wally!" was next. Mom followed Carol, and I followed Mom.

When I joined them Wally was lying on the ground, his wheel-chair overturned, I never got a good look at what Wally had been yelling at, but Oberon was pursuing whatever it was. Carol and Mom were tending to Wally, so I started after Oberon.

"Stay here, Jasper," ordered Mom.

Reluctantly I stopped, but I watched Oberon disappear over a ridge. It was a marvel to see him run. He wasn't fast, but he was smooth. It was mesmerizing to watch a man his size run smoothly.

"What was that?" I asked.

Wally was sitting up on the ground when he answered, "I don't know. I didn't see it knock me over, and while I was lying there, it kept head-butting me."

Carol was kneeling next to him, squeezing him in different places looking for wounds.

"Are you hurt?" asked Mom.

"I don't think so," said Wally, patting and squeezing in the same manner Carol had done.

Carol was no longer kneeling next to her husband. She was standing rigidly, mouth open, eyes bulging, fixated on the ridge Oberon had crossed over. Mom and Wally noticed her as well.

Standing next to her, Mom put a hand on her back and gently said, "Carol, are you alright?"

"No!" screamed Carol, pointing at something the rest of us could not see.

"No!" screamed Carol again. This time she held her hands over her face and bent over.

"What did you see?" asked Mom in a tone that sounded more like an order than the compassion I would have expected.

Carol was surprised by Mom's tone, too. Staying bent over, Carol looked up at Mom with scrunched-up eyes.

"What did you see?" repeated Mom in a softened but still firm tone.

"Dogs," said Carol meekly, "or pigs. I don't know which. But there were a bunch of them, and they were chasing Oberon. It was like it was real."

Mom stepped closer to her. "It was real, Carol. It was a vision." Turning Carol's head back toward the ridge she said, "I know it's scary, but if Oberon is in trouble, you have to try and see."

"I don't know how," pleaded Carol, resisting Mom's hands on her head.

"You do know," said Mom. "You're afraid, but we're running out of time. Now, just look."

Carol stood up straighter, swallowed hard, and stared off in the direction she had stared before, her forehead flinching. "I can't see him. He's under the awning."

The awning is a rock formation half a mile beyond the ridge that borders the eastern edge of our farm. My late brother, Linus had named it "the awning" when he was in junior high. It was a great place for shelter if it rained when he camped out.

"There's about a dozen of those dog things trapping him in there." Her head jerked back.

"What happened?" asked Mom. She wasn't looking at Carol. She was looking at the northern end of the ridgeline and moving her finger like she was directing traffic.

"Two of them charged him, but they backed off. One flew

backward out from under the awning, like he had been kicked. The other slunk out."

The next thing I knew, Aiden and Maire were standing next to us. I didn't know they were there until Aiden said, "There they are."

I followed his eyes to the east where a dozen wolves were sprinting along the ridgeline.

"They're getting ready to attack him again," Carol cried out. She was pointing again. "They've split up. They're going to attack him from two directions!"

The wolves disappeared beyond the ridge.

"No!" screamed Carol, hiding her eyes again with her hands.

"Did they attack?" asked Aiden.

"I don't know," said Carol. "I just suddenly felt like I was falling." She stood up again and opened her eyes. "It's a hyena," she said. "I'm looking right into its face." She looked at Mom. "What are hyenas doing here?"

"Keep watching, Carol," Mom told her.

Carol frowned at her but obeyed. "They keep charging him and backing off."

"They're wearing him down," explained Aiden.

"No!" Carol yelled again. "One just attacked him, under the awning. He's out. Another one is charging him from the other side." She lunged forward. "They're all going in now. He's down! He's down!"

Mom put her arm around Carol's shoulder.

"The wolves are arriving. Thank God."

Mom put her hand on Carol's cheek, turning her head away. "You don't have to watch anymore."

Carol's eyes were so wide, I don't think she could have closed them if she wanted to. "What's happening to me, Mama?" she pleaded.

Mom slowly rubbed Carol's cheek with her hand and said, "You were having a vision."

I don't know what a vision is or what it's supposed to do to you, but I do know this: when Mom told Carol she was having a vision, she wasn't telling the truth.

CHAPTER 7

SUNDAY MORNING

I HAD WOKEN UP EARLY IN HOPES of having the conversation with my mom that was postponed due to the hyena attack the day before. I sat at the table playing *Call of Duty* until ten o'clock, when Mom finally came in. She hadn't even sat down before Maggie came in behind her. Maggie had been tending to Oberon, who was recuperating in our guest room.

"How is he?" asked Mom.

"Nothing is broken, but there are bruises and bites and scratches all over him. He is sound asleep, but his breathing is strained. If that is the extent of his injuries, then he'll just need a few days of rest," answered Maggie.

Mom squinted and leaned toward Maggie. "What aren't you saying?"

Maggie immediately looked at me.

"You can speak in front of him," Mom told her. "He's already been exposed to plenty." She looked at me and added, "And I think he's going to keep pushing until he understands everything."

I nodded yes. I felt some relief because it sounded like she intended to answer my questions.

"Yes, Mother," said Maggie. It was the first time I had ever heard Aunt Maggie address my mother that way.

"If Aayma had anything to do with those beasts, then I fear they might be rabid," said Maggie sternly.

"It is what she would do," agreed Mom. She looked at me again and sighed. "I wish we had ended this in Hendersonville."

"So you think it is Aayma?" asked Maggie.

"I can think of no other explanation," confessed Mom. "Is Oberon feverish?"

"No," said Maggie. "Does that matter?"

"I would think he'd be feverish if he were infected with rabies."

"If he was a man," countered Maggie. "Do you know what he is?"

"He's not a man?" questioned Mom. Her face contorted in a look of confusion I had never seen.

"No," said Maggie, looking equally confused. "Did you not call him into service?"

Mom shook her head no and then collapsed into a kitchen chair.

Maggie lunged forward and caught her before she fell forward off the chair.

"Oh," said Mom weakly. "I don't know what happened."

"You're burning up," said Maggie. She looked at me and asked, "Do you know what happened to her? She is feverish."

I looked at my mother's left hand. It was red and swollen.

When Maggie followed my eyes she lifted Mom's hand and asked, "What kind of bite is this?"

"She said she was a black mamba," I told her, remembering Victoria Rasnake. "She bit that detective was following us, and he died almost right away." I was standing next to Mom, but I didn't know what to do to help. "She said she was fine," I pleaded. "She said it wouldn't hurt her."

"It shouldn't have," said Maggie.

"It was a black mamba," said Mom while inhaling deeply and struggling to keep her eyes open. "I am fine. I just got a little dizzy."

"You're not fine," argued Maggie, "and you're going back to bed."

"I am not," said Mom stiffening her back.

"You are, and you can't stop us," said Maggie, cupping her hand under Mom's left arm. She pointed for me to do the same with the other arm.

"I am fine," said Mom as we lifted her to her feet. "We have too many things to discuss for me to return to bed," she told us as we led her to her bedroom.

Once we had her sitting on her bed, Maggie looked at me and said, "You should excuse us now."

As I left Mom's room I heard Maggie tell her, "You know as well as I do that we are perfectly safe until nightfall."

CHAPTER 8

SAYING GOOD-BYE

I NEVER THOUGHT I'D BE DISAPPOINTED to see Riley, but I was. While I waited for Maggie in the kitchen, Riley and her father parked in front of the truck that was still stationed in the middle of our compound. I desperately wanted to see Riley, but I was feeling desperation for several reasons right then.

I watched through the kitchen door as King opened his trunk and removed a briefcase. Riley stayed in the passenger seat of his Grand Marquis. She had sunglasses on, and her head was stooped forward. At first I was glad Riley hadn't seen me watching her. I had some questions for Maggie and I didn't want to wait to ask, but then it dawned on me that Riley was crying.

"Hey," I said, tapping on her window a moment later.

She looked up at me without rolling the window down right away. She smiled, but it was the sorriest smile I had ever seen.

"What's wrong?" I asked through the window.

The door popped open. I moved out of the way while she stepped out of the car.

"Oh, Jasper," she whimpered as she took a hold of me around my neck.

She was holding me so tightly that I could hardly move my head. As best I could I looked at her father. He was watching us

35

from behind the car. His smile was sorry, too, as he looked down and away.

"We're leaving," she said. It sounded like she was holding her breath.

I tried to pull my head back so that I could see her, but she wouldn't let go of my neck. "You're leaving," I repeated.

I could feel her head nod yes against my neck.

"When?" I asked frantically. "Why?"

I could feel her take a big breath, and I heard her sigh as she let go of me. She looked at her father and said, "Jasper and I are going to take a walk, okay?"

"I don't know, honey," King said. He was frowning.

"It is safe," Maggie told him.

I don't know how long Maggie had been standing there. I also didn't know how safe it was to go for a walk. Yesterday Wally had been attacked just behind the birthing barn, and Oberon just a half mile over the ridge. When I looked at Maggie she was staring directly at me.

"It is safe," Maggie repeated to me.

Riley and I walked in the woods to the west of our farm. We just held hands and walked until we got to the creek.

"This was my favorite wading spot," I told her when we stopped.

Riley looked at it for a moment and then took off her sandals. "Let's wade."

It was a warm day for mid-April, but it wasn't summer. "That water's going to be freezing," I told her.

She stepped in anyway. If the cold bothered her, she didn't show it.

I stayed where I was, on the grass. "You said you were leaving," I reminded her.

"My father thinks I won't be safe here anymore," she said.

"I've argued with him ever since I got back, but his mind is made up. I thought he was changing his mind last night when a detective came over. I think her name was Nina Charles. She's the one who came to get me when we were driving back from Hendersonville. She told him that the people who took me are all dead now. It was that guy who used to work for my dad and those tall men."

They aren't all dead, I thought, but I realized the police wouldn't know about Aayma.

"He just wants to be sure," I said, defending her father. I didn't want her to go, but I wanted her to be safe even more.

Riley kicked at the water. "I know. As soon as the detective left, our doorbell rang. I thought it was the detective again, but it wasn't. There was note stuck to the door with a knife."

"What did it say?"

Riley stiffened and looked directly at me. "'It isn't over,'" she answered, pronouncing each word distinctly.

It would have made sense for me to ask what that meant right then, but I thought I already knew what it meant. It was the lab that my sister—disease—really wanted to put an end to, which meant none of us were safe.

"Where are you going?" is what I asked.

"Richmond," she answered. "My father has a sister there. He already has me enrolled in a private school."

I looked down. I think if I had kept looking at her I would have cried. I didn't want to cry.

"Jasper!" Riley yelled.

I looked up just in time to see her standing next to me, clutching at my arm. She was trying to lead me back toward the house. Her eyes were fixated on something to my right.

It was a wolf, just watching us. I was pretty sure it was Malcolm, who was the first wolf to be nice to me. Without taking his eyes off us, he dipped his head down and took a drink from the creek.

"We're okay," I told her. I retrieved my left arm from her grasp and put it around her.

Pointing with my right hand I said, "Do you see how he's standing? He's just watching. If he were a threat he'd be more tense." I don't know if that was true or not, but I wanted to comfort her.

"Is he . . . one of yours?"

"No," I said immediately. "He's not mine. But he's one of the wolves that protected me before."

Riley put her palm against my chest and felt for the wolf's-tooth necklace. She smiled when she felt it through my shirt.

"Look," I said, pointing to our left where two more wolves were standing and watching us.

She squeezed me around the middle as she saw them.

"They're beautiful," she said.

"Yes."

"Are you a little scared?" she asked.

"I'm scared of losing you," I confessed.

CHAPTER 9

MAGGIE'S SURPRISE

A HALF HOUR LATER I WAS STANDING by myself, watching Riley's father back away. Neither Riley nor I waved. We just watched each other get smaller. I could feel my chin start to quiver, and I knew if I tried to move I'd break down. So I just stood there looking at the last spot where I could see her.

"Jasper," whispered Carol. She was standing next to me with her arm around my shoulder. "Riley's a real nice girl. She'll be back."

"I know," I said. "I just wish it was different." Looking at Carol I added, "I wish a lot of things were different." I think I was hoping she knew more than she knew, but there was no sign of that.

"When you're ready, Maggie wants us. Mom's asking for us."

"Mom's up?" I asked.

"I assume," said Carol. "We haven't been to the big house yet. Wally and I were going over some papers with Dr. Lyons. There're some loose ends with the sale of his business that he needs Wally to take care of."

I nodded.

She leaned closer to me and said, "He's not selling their house."

39

I didn't understand why she told me that, but she explained, "That means he's planning on coming back."

Mom was on her bed, looking pale and glassy-eyed. Even the small movement to look in our direction seemed like a struggle for her. She winced as she tried to lift her head. Her appearance was very unsettling, but I was at least a bit prepared for it. Carol stopped breathing and froze just inside Mom's bedroom door. Maggie had to direct her to a chair next to the bed.

Mom reached out her hand, and Carol took hold of it. Her movement was rigid and seemed to exhaust her. Her eyes were open wide with an expression of shock, but at the same time she was crying.

"What's wrong, Mama?" Carol asked.

"She's weak," said Maggie, circling to the other side of the bed. "She's been poisoned. She needs time to fight it off." Maggie reached across Mom and tipped her head to the side. Wiping Mom's cheek Maggie said, "She is working the poison out through her tears and her saliva and her sweat."

"We need to get her to a hospital!" said Carol, standing back up.

"Please sit," Maggie told her.

"We've got to move her now," Carol begged.

"Sit down!" ordered Maggie more forcefully.

When Carol looked down at Mom, Mom blinked yes. I did the same when she looked at me. Carol was reluctant, but she sat.

"Thank you," said Maggie. "Now listen, child. What I need to tell you is going to be hard to believe, but you must hear it all."

"What's going on?" asked Carol, her face a knot of tension.

"Just listen," I told her.

"What do you know about all this?" Carol asked me accusingly.

"I know a little more than you, I think," I told her, "but I don't know enough to make sense of any of it."

"What do you know?" demanded Carol, standing back up.

"I don't know, but I think we're in trouble," I said, looking at Maggie for confirmation.

Maggie nodded.

"We!" repeated Carol.

"Our family," I said.

Carol looked at Maggie, who nodded her agreement, and said, "Please sit."

Carol sat back down and scooted her chair closer to Mom's bed. She had been holding Mom's hand the entire time, but now she held it with both hands.

"Thank you," said Maggie. She and Mom locked eyes for a moment before Mom nodded at her. "Your mother is Mother Nature."

Judging by Carol's lack of reaction, I'd say she heard what Maggie told her, but it didn't sink in. When she was in high school she and her friends used to refer to Mom as "Earth Mother," so she probably heard it in a similar fashion.

"Your mother," continued Maggie, "has dominion over nature."

Carol frowned and again said, "We've got to get Mom to the hospital."

Maggie held up a finger. "I will show you." She turned her back to us and began taking off her dress.

"What are you doing?" shouted Carol.

With the dress off Maggie was completely naked. Instead of answering Carol she just collapsed. She was completely out of sight.

Carol stood up again to see over the edge of the bed. I leaned in that direction, too.

Maggie leaped up on the bed next to Mom. She sat, perched regally on her hind end, staring directly into Carol's eyes—only it wasn't Aunt Maggie anymore. It was a black panther, with a shiny black coat and a piercing stare.

Carol let go of Mom's hand and collapsed back into the chair.

"I thought that would be the faster way to convince her," said Maggie, standing, in her human form, next to Carol.

"We'll know in a minute," I said, because I could see Carol already returning to consciousness.

When she could focus, she found Maggie leaning over her nearly eyeball to eyeball. Carol flinched away and piled her hands on top of her heart. "Oh my," she exhaled. "Was I asleep?"

"You weren't asleep, Carol," I said. "You fainted."

Carol rubbed her head. "You wouldn't believe the dream I just had."

"It wasn't a dream, darling," said Maggie.

Carol frowned. In a squeaky voice she asked, "Maggie, why don't you have any clothes on?"

CHAPTER 10

TELLING CAROL

CAROL ACCEPTED THAT A HOSPITAL for normal humans was not the place for our mother. Surely she was as worried about Mom as I was, but in the end we had to continue to trust that if Aunt Maggie said Mom just needed rest, then that's what we should do. Why should the discovery that Maggie's a scary predatory feline change how trustworthy she was? I wouldn't say Carol understood. For that matter, I wouldn't say I understood either, but there were things to tend to and it was time to move on.

Carol spent the afternoon watching Mom and trying to make sense of everything she'd heard and seen.

Maggie shuttled back and forth between Mom's and Oberon's rooms. The most recent status report was that each was sleeping soundly, which was what they both needed.

I spent the day unloading the truck with Dirk and Evans, while Wally supervised where everything went. We had to use a ramp to get that big crate out. When we were done, Wally gave each of us a fifty-dollar bill. I was directed to use mine to pay for pizza and soda, but I was in no mood for that.

Giving my fifty-dollar bill to Dirk I said, "You guys take it. I need to hang here."

Dirk took the money and nodded while shaking my hand.

"Thanks for helping," I said.

"No prob," he said and headed to his car.

"We'll return the truck," announced Evans. Leaning toward me he quietly added, "You're spent, Jasper. It's Riley, isn't it?"

I'm sure Harlan must have known and told him because I hadn't mentioned it. A shrug was the best answer I could give him, but it was enough. He put his hand on my shoulder and rocked me back and forth once. "I've got your back anytime, man."

I know Evans meant he had my back when he said it, but there was no way he could have known what we were facing or what having my back might mean.

"I know," I told him. "Thanks."

"Hungry?" asked Carol when I entered the kitchen. She was at the counter chopping peanuts.

"Tuna fish?" I asked, grabbing a handful of peanuts she hadn't chopped yet. Carol's tuna fish recipe included chopped peanuts and grapes, which she'd spread over toast and then melt Gouda cheese on top of it. I liked it, but I wouldn't have bothered chopping up the peanuts.

"How long have you known?" she asked while continuing to chop.

"Known what?" I countered.

Glaring at me she firmly said, "Do I look like I'm in a joking mood?" She waved the knife in my direction. "You know what I'm asking you. I don't want to be protected like a little child anymore."

I raised my hands. "Only a couple of weeks, I swear. Do you remember when I almost got killed and messed my shoulder up?"

She nodded yes.

"Well, it was a couple of days after that." I put my hands down. "And after that, Riley got kidnapped, and it's been nuts since then."

"It's still nuts, if you ask me," sighed Carol. She put the knife down and leaned forward on the counter. "Does what happened to Wally have anything to do with what happened to Mom?" After a pause she added, "Or what happened to Oberon?" After another pause she looked at me again and added, "Or you?"

"I think so," I answered.

Carol stood up and turned around so that her back was against the edge of the counter. Folding her arms she said, "Look, Jasper. I'm tired and I don't know enough to know what to ask, so please, start from the beginning and tell me everything you know."

"I'll tell you what I know, but ever since I got back from Hendersonville I've been waiting to ask Mom a bunch of questions of my own, so it's not going to be complete."

"Anything you could tell me would be better than what my imagination is doing to me," confessed Carol.

"For me," I began, "it started the night Mrs. Dietrich came over to talk to Mom about Dr. Dietrich's death. She couldn't get anyone to believe that he was murdered, but Mom believed her and told her she'd see justice was done."

"What does that mean?"

"I didn't know at the time, but what it meant was that Mom was going to get her servants to see that justice was done."

"Servants?" repeated Carol. "What kind of servants does Mom have?"

"Well, Aiden Carmac and Maire are Mom's servants," I answered.

Carol frowned. "'Servants' is a weird word, Jasper. They're detectives Mom hired, not servants."

"They're wolves," I said.

She tipped her head to the right and squinted.

"They are wolves," I said again.

45

"Of course," said Carol, raising her eyebrows. "Mom's Mother Nature, Maggie's a panther, so of course the detectives are wolves. And the hyenas are chipmunks, right?"

"That would be nice," I said, "but probably not."

"Continue," she said with a flip of her hand.

"I thought it was all over when Mr. Benjamin disappeared. That's when Aiden told me who Mom really is."

"Aiden the wolf?" said Carol.

"Yes. He's the white one. He and the pack had been watching out for me for a while. I just didn't know it until after that. And then everything seemed great for a while. Riley's dad gave me that car and offered me that job."

"I remember that part," said Carol.

"And then it all went batty when Riley was kidnapped." I wasn't sure how to continue after that.

I don't know if I wobbled, but Carol noticed something and said, "Let's sit."

We sat across from each other at the kitchen table. I took a deep breath and began again. "We thought Riley was the target because she was the one taken and because her father got that threat about selling Lion Pharmaceuticals." I flipped my hands over. "I guess that was part of it, but I think I might have been the target, too."

"You? Why you?"

"This is where it gets hard to believe," I said.

She laughed, but it wasn't laughter. It was a single laugh that sort of exploded out of her mouth. "Oh, *this* is where it gets hard to believe."

I just stared at her.

"You're serious," she said, reaching across the table to put her hand on top of mine. She was wide-eyed.

"Maybe you should let this soak in before I tell you more," I suggested.

She held up her hands. "You're really scaring me now, but keep going. Whatever it is, I need to know it."

"Okay," I said. "The people who took Riley weren't really people. Mostly they were vultures, but one of them was a poisonous snake, a black mamba."

"Wait a minute," said Carol. "Mom can make people out of wolves, right? She's Mother Nature, right?"

"Yeah."

"Well, what's with the vultures? Can't Mom just zap them or something?" asked Carol.

"Look, Carol, I'm not sure how this all works. Maybe we can ask Maggie about it later. But I don't think the snake or the vultures were Mom's servants. They were following the orders of a woman named Aayma." I looked long and hard at Carol before adding, "We've seen her before."

"What?" she asked, the alarm in her voice was strong.

"Do you remember that time when I was about ten and you took me to the post office?"

She shrugged.

"You were inside and there was this woman, she had red hair and green eyes, and a man was trying to take her purse and I got out of the car and helped her."

"Yes," Carol said, "I remember that. You nearly got knocked out."

"That was her," I said.

"Who was what?"

"That redheaded woman from the post office is the same woman who had Riley kidnapped. She was controlling the snake that bit Mom. She was controlling the vultures that took Riley.

I'd bet anything she was controlling the hyenas that attacked Wally and Oberon, too."

"Who is she, and why is she doing this?" said Carol, half whining and half pleading.

"I'm not sure about the why, Carol, but the who is pretty hard to take."

Carol just stared at me.

"Her name is Aayma, and she is disease," I said as matter-of-factly as I could.

"She is . . . disease," repeated Carol.

"I don't know what it means either, but I do know this. She knows all about our family, and when I asked Mom who she was, Mom said—" I couldn't quite finish that sentence right away. It just didn't sound right in my head.

"What?" asked Carol. "What did Mom say?"

"When I asked Mom who Aayma is, she said"—I still felt a choking in my throat, but I forced out—"Mom said, 'She's my daughter.'"

CHAPTER 11

THE ENCOUNTER

CAROL STILL HAD THE BLANK STARE on her face when Maggie returned to Mom's room. Maggie took one look at her, and then turning to me said, "You explained about your mother."

"I did," I admitted. "And Aayma."

Looking back at Carol, Maggie put her arms around Carol's head and drew her to Maggie's midsection. "That is quite a lot for you to take all at once, darling."

Carol leaned into Maggie and hugged her back. They stayed like that until a moan and restless turn from Mom snapped them back into action.

Maggie leaned over Mom, wiping drool from her cheek.

Carol circled Mom's bed. Leaning on the opposite side of the bed from Maggie, she watched Maggie take care of Mom.

From the end of the bed I asked, "Isn't there anything else we can do?"

Maggie shook her head no. "She must fight this within herself. And she is fighting." Standing up, Maggie looked at Carol first and then me. "She has no energy for anything else. Her body must do its work, and we must do ours."

"Our work?" repeated Carol. "What's our work?"

"Yeah," I agreed. "Just tell us what to do."

Maggie looked at me immediately and answered, "It is not for me to tell you what you must do, but I think you already know what your calling is. And I think you know what some of your gifts are. You must let that knowledge inform you about what to do."

"My gifts!" I repeated. "Do you mean my sense of smell?"

Maggie didn't answer. She just stared across Mom's bed at Carol.

"What's a calling?" I asked.

Again Maggie didn't answer. She stayed locked in on Carol, who had risen to her feet and looked back at Maggie with her mouth slightly open and her forehead a knot of tension.

I was getting frustrated that Maggie had left me hanging and wasn't answering my question, but this was clearly not the time to push it.

"I don't think I can take any more surprises," said Carol. Her voice was high and weak.

"I know, darling," Maggie told her.

They stood like that, watching each other silently again until it was time for Maggie to wipe Mom's cheek again.

"Do you know this woman who is responsible for poisoning Mom?" asked Carol.

"I do."

"Jasper says she is our sister," Carol said in a firmer voice.

Maggie looked at me, then back at Carol. "She is."

"Why is she doing this to us?"

Maggie's eyes flexed as she leaned against the bed. She looked down at Mom for a moment before saying, "I do not know the answer to your question, but I think it is the right question and I think we must find the answer."

"We," repeated Carol, her high, weak voice returning.

I did not see what happened next. Maggie and Carol went to

the open pasture at the far back end of our property, a pasture about the size of a football field that we hadn't needed to enclose. Beyond that pasture was a wooded area. They went to that open pasture to find an answer to Carol's question. How that would answer the question, I was not to discover until later. I was told that I was not invited to join them. My protests did nothing to change Maggie's insistence that this was her and Carol's job to do and I would only be in the way.

Needless to say, I was angry at being left out, but I was given the responsibility of caring for Mom and Oberon in their absence. I resolved to set my anger aside until they returned.

Caring for Mom and Oberon meant going back and forth between the two rooms and checking to see if anything ever changed. I don't know what I would have done if something did change, but luckily it didn't. I wiped cheeks, listened to labored breathing, and fluffed pillows.

"How are the patients?" asked Maggie. I don't know how long they had been sitting at the kitchen table, but it had only been about fifteen minutes since I walked from Mom's room to Oberon's room, so it could not have been very long.

"No change," I answered.

Carol was sitting at the table staring at her hands. Looking at her I wondered if she had been hypnotized or something. "Are you okay?" I asked.

"We have to leave," said Carol. Other than her lips, nothing else moved when she answered.

I looked at Maggie, hoping she'd explain, but she just said, "Sit with your sister. I will see to the patients."

I sat across from Carol and waited for her to make the first move. Raising her head slowly she studied my face. At first I wondered if she recognized me, but then I thought she was thinking through what to say to me.

When she was ready she took a deep breath and told me the story of her encounter with Aayma.

Carol and Maggie walked through the back pasture where Kitty was tending to her flock. Once they were through the back gate and in the open pasture Maggie said, "We'll wait here."

Carol asked, "Wait here for what?"

"Her," answered Maggie, looking straight into the forest on the other side of the pasture.

Carol said she couldn't see what Maggie was looking at until a pale redheaded woman walked out away from the trees. Carol knew right away it was Aayma, describing the woman as tall and shapely, wearing tight jeans and a black sleeveless V-necked shirt.

As Aayma began walking across the field, first one, then three more hyenas joined her.

"Leave your pets," shouted Maggie.

Aayma stopped and grinned as the hyenas caught up to her. She and Maggie stared at each other as the hyenas milled around her, sneering at them.

Kitty had her paws up on the top rail of the fence, barking as loudly as she could.

Finally Aayma looked down and said something Carol couldn't hear. Then, waving her hand, she sent the hyenas back to the edge of the woods and continued walking toward them.

Carol told me that when she turned around to tend to Kitty, Kitty immediately got frantic. Then when Carol turned back around, Aayma was standing right next to her.

"She's not as pretty as I expected," Aayma said to Maggie.

"What do you want, Aayma?" snarled Maggie.

"I want what is mine," Aayma said, still looking only at Carol. "Your hair is all wrong, dear. Don't you think you'd look better as a blonde?" She took hold of a strand of Carol's hair and lifted it away. With a curl in her lip she added, "Don't you use conditioner?"

"Don't touch me," snapped Carol, swatting her hair out of Aayma's hand.

Laughing, Aayma stepped over to the fence and looked at the back of Carol's house. "Your husband is in there now, is he not?"

"That's none of your business," answered Carol.

"He's setting up a research lab, is he not?"

"None of your business."

Aayma laughed again. Turning toward Carol, Aayma said, "You know, dear, you really have no idea what my business is, and furthermore—" As she said it, her face contorted angrily and she leaned toward Carol.

At that same moment Maggie stepped between them.

Aayma snorted and stepped back, her face returning to its cover-girl state. "And furthermore," Aayma continued, "you have no idea what your business is either."

"What do you *want*, Aayma?" demanded Maggie.

"I want her and her husband as far from my brother as possible," spewed Aayma.

"What?" blurted Carol. "Why?"

"You know why," answered Aayma.

"I don't know anything," said Carol. That's what Carol said, but I think that was her telling me her impressions of the story, rather than what she actually said to Aayma at the time.

"How is Mommy?" Aayma asked. She was leaning on the fence with her fingers curled over the top rail. The answer she got was a nip from Kitty that drew blood from her ring finger. Aayma stared hard at Kitty, the anger glaring, as she put her finger in her mouth.

"The Mother is fine," said Maggie.

Aayma stepped away from the fence. Laughing again she said, "Really? And she's so fine that she sent you and Bo-Peep here to do her talking." She smirked. "That doesn't sound like Mommy."

"Don't call her that!" snapped Carol.

Leaning menacingly toward Carol again Aayma said, "You think you can tell me what to do." She waved across the pasture toward the forest, "We could overrun this place anytime we wanted."

Maggie, still between Carol and Aayma, leaned forward herself. In a deeper voice and with a slower cadence she said, "Do it now."

Aayma stared back and then looked beyond them to the woods to the left of the open pasture. There, just on the edge of the pasture, were a dozen wolves. They were pacing and watching. To the right of the pasture was a six-foot berm that ran along that side of our property. On top of the berm were another dozen wolves pacing and watching.

After surveying the field Aayma smiled and said, "Not now, but just see to it that one of Mommy's kids finds their way out of town." With that she walked across the pasture, and with the hyenas following, she disappeared into the forest without looking back.

CHAPTER 12

CAROL'S PLAN

WHEN CAROL WAS FINISHED, SHE ASKED, "And she told you she is our sister?"

"She didn't tell me that," I clarified. "Mom told me that. She told me things about us that made me believe she's known us for a long time. She told me about Dad and the wolf's-tooth necklace."

"And she's disease," said Carol, eyebrows raised.

"That is what Aiden told me, but he said it in front of Mom, so it has to be right."

With a sarcastic bob of her head Carol shrugged and said, "Of course it's right, but what does it mean? Come on, Jasper, tell me. You've been dealing with this for a while. What does it mean for a person"—she snorted—"a sister I didn't know about until thirty minutes ago . . . what does it mean for her to be disease?"

"I don't know."

"How could you not know?" She was angry.

"I'm just a kid," I said. "I was going to ask Mom when I could talk to her, but you know about that."

Carol reached across the table and held her hands open to me.

When I took hold of them she gave a squeeze and said, "I'm sorry, Jasper. That wasn't fair. This has just really thrown me."

"It's thrown us all," I said, squeezing back.

Carol's eyes pooled up. "It just seems like everything was so perfect just a little while ago. Wally loved his job. I loved mine. We were here with my family." Her grip tightened. "I don't know how it could have gotten this crazy this fast. And Jasper," she shook my hands back and forth, "who in the world could we talk to about all this? Who'd believe us?"

I just shrugged my shoulders.

"Does Riley know about any of this? Does her dad know about it?"

I shook my head no.

Letting go of my hands she stood up from the table and stood at the back door looking at her home through the kitchen door. "We have to leave," she announced. "I'm going to have to tell Wally to pack up the lab and start looking for a job somewhere else. He's not going to want to go without an explanation." She huffed through her nose, "How am I going to explain that?"

I didn't think she was expecting an answer, so I didn't bother telling her I didn't have one.

Turning around to face me again, she continued, "But I'm not leaving until Mom gets better, so that means you're leaving."

"What?" Suddenly I was more in the conversation than I had been the moment before.

"We can't stay together, Jasper. Aayma said she would overrun this place if we didn't separate."

"That is not exactly what she said," said Maggie from behind me.

"She said she could," clarified Carol. "That was a threat."

"It was a threat," agreed Maggie, "but she would not dare to attempt something like that against the Mother."

Carol moved to the middle of the kitchen. Her eyebrows were

knit together, and she was pointing toward our mother's room. "She already has, Maggie. Mom is really sick."

"She will get better," stated Maggie firmly.

Putting her hands on her hips Carol said, "I hope so. I hate the thought that she might not, but she might not, and we have to face that."

"Listen, child," said Maggie, her voice soft and calm. "This is one of the differences between you and us. Humans can think of possibilities that are not possible." She glanced at me and continued. "Humans can worry themselves sick thinking of possibilities that are not possible."

"Mom might not get better," Carol said flatly.

"That is not a possibility I can imagine. Nor do I want to."

Carol took a deep breath and began to say something, but thought better of it. With a slump and a sigh she admitted, "I don't want to imagine it either." As she sat back down across from me she said, "But we need to have a plan until Mom gets better."

"Yes, we do," agreed Maggie.

Looking back at me Carol said, "That means you're leaving, Jasper."

"Oh, no, I'm not," I said. The thought of leaving Boone while Mom was still sick made me sick. "I'm not leaving Mom now either."

Carol's eyes pooled up. "Please, Jasper. It's just temporary. It will buy us time to figure something out."

We stared at each other.

"You can go to Richmond if you want," she offered.

That was tempting for a moment. Being there while Riley was there was appealing, but then I thought about Mom again.

"Think about Mom, Jasper," said Carol.

"I *am* thinking about Mom."

"You're thinking about you. Think about what happens to Mom if you don't leave and that woman tries to overrun this place." Carol looked closely at me as I digested what she said. "Without Mom's help, we are not up for an all-out confrontation."

My thoughts were all over the place. It felt good to think about going where Riley was, but whenever I had those thoughts I immediately felt selfish, like I was abandoning Mom. Not leaving, though, was a threat to everyone, including Mom. Besides, there was really nothing I could do but be here to help.

"Just until we have a plan," I said finally.

When Maggie returned to the kitchen I was sitting alone at the table. I was more numb than lost in thought as my feelings bounced around inside me like a pinball. I felt frightened that we were being threatened, but that would morph into anger. Anger wouldn't last long before it became sadness. The thought of losing Mom was never so close or so real. I couldn't sit with the sadness for long, so I'd flip into thoughts of heading to Richmond with Riley, but as soon as those thoughts took shape I felt guilty for having them. What was going on inside of me was moving so fast that I didn't notice Maggie's return.

Maggie sat next to me and said, "Tell me what you noticed about Oberon."

It took me a moment to get her question into focus and then I remembered what I had thought as I sat with him while Carol and Maggie were out with Aayma. "I don't think he's human," I said. "But I don't know what he is. Do you know what he is?"

Maggie shook her head no. "What did you notice about his sweating and his breathing?"

"I don't know," I said. "He's sweating a lot, but he's huge."

"What does it mean, Maggie?" asked Carol, returning from down the hall.

"It means he is getting better. It is a reason to be hopeful."

"Good," said Carol. "I needed a reason to be hopeful."

The immediate plan was to send me away somewhere while Carol convinced Wally to leave Boone. This, Carol believed, would appease Aayma enough to leave us alone until Mom was well. She reasoned that the combination of Wally's skill and my nose was a threat to disease, and if the threat to Aayma were relieved, then Aayma's threat to us would be relieved as well. And although I didn't like leaving Mom right then, the thought of going somewhere was very appealing, especially if I could go where Riley went.

Maggie didn't agree but acquiesced. "We should not surrender territory because of a mere threat," she told us. "If defeated, move on and make the best of it, but to move on, an interloper must prove the threat first."

"That sounds good," said Carol, "but it is more complicated than that for humans. We move on for all sorts of reasons. Wally and I moved here from California."

"California was never your home. You returned here because this is your home. Aayma wants to take it from you. Can you make another place home, or will your heart always yearn to return?"

I could tell Maggie was getting to Carol because Carol's response was, "I don't care. I won't risk my mother or my husband."

"You are afraid," said Maggie.

"Of course I am," said Carol, "and I have good reason to be."

"You do," agreed Maggie. "Fear is a good ally, but it is not an alpha."

"What do you think, Jasper?" asked Carol.

"If I went to Richmond it would be to buy us time," I said. "It wouldn't be to move on. Maybe I could finish the semester in Richmond and Wally could disassemble the lab. Who knows? Maybe that would be enough for Aayma."

"Yes!" agreed Carol enthusiastically. "That's perfect."

"It's agreed then," I said, already thinking about heading off to Richmond.

"I have to talk to Wally," said Carol as she stood.

I stood up also and said, "I have to pack."

Carol was at the kitchen door, and I was nearly down the hall when we realized that Maggie had not moved.

"Are we agreed?" Carol asked her.

Looking at Carol, Maggie said, "It is your decision. I had my say, and I accept what you have decided." To me she added, "You may find that that lab is more your territory than you thought."

CHAPTER 13

MONDAY MORNING

I'D HAVE LEFT MONDAY MORNING, but there were more details about transferring schools and relocating than I thought. I had my own car, so just getting to Richmond was covered. Maggie knew someone in Richmond I could stay with, so that was covered. Because Mom did so much traveling as an author Maggie was already listed as a guardian, so Maggie could sign transfer and registration papers. All I had to do was clear it all with my school counselor, Mr. Gabriel.

Before first period I dropped by Mr. Gabriel's office to set up an appointment. He was sitting at his desk reading from what looked like a beat-up old book.

"Can I come by during second period?" I asked from his open doorway.

Leaning to his right he ran his finger across his open appointment book. He tapped the place he stopped and looked up, "Sorry, Jasper, I'm already committed then. How about right after lunch?"

That was during my lit class, but I was leaving, so what difference did it make? "Perfect," I said.

"What's up?"

"I need to talk about transferring."

"Oh, my," he said, standing up. "We'll be sorry to see you go. Is everything alright?"

I was tempted to tell him that my family was sending me away because of a threat from disease, but I knew better. "Everything's fine."

He nodded. "That's good. Where are you headed?"

"Richmond." I was a little surprised and even more disappointed that he didn't just assume that I'd be going where Riley went. It would be the first thought of any of my friends.

He smiled. "I meant what school. We'll need the name of the school to send your transcript."

"I'll get it," I told him and headed off to class.

The day went painfully slowly. Every time I looked for the time I thought, *This time tomorrow I'll be in Richmond.* I'm sure that didn't help the time pass faster, but I couldn't help it.

Lunch was different. I wanted to surprise Riley, so the only person I told that I was leaving was Harlan, and I only did that so that she could text Riley and find out what school she was going to.

I got my usual two hamburgers for lunch, but because it was my last day at Watauga for a while, I also got some of Ms. Pitino's banana pudding. She layers her banana pudding in clear plastic cups while it's still warm, putting a few chocolate chips between the layers. The chocolate melts a little. It's wonderful, but I had agreed with my junior high counselor that I would avoid sweets during the day because of my ADD. But it was my last day and I didn't really plan on sticking around past my meeting with Mr. Gabriel, so I decided to indulge.

Harlan was waving at me when I entered the dining hall. I could see that everyone was there, including Evans, Dirk, and Cathy. Evans had become a fixture at our table since Hendersonville, but Dirk and Cathy usually ate at the football table. I assumed Harlan had told them I was leaving.

Dirk and Evans were sitting across from each other at one end of the table. The seat at the end next to them was empty, so I sat there.

"Is that whipped, or what?" Dirk said to Evans without a glance in my direction.

Evans nodded, "That's whipped alright."

I was right. Harlan had told them.

"Have you ever been to Richmond?" asked Alice from the other end of the table. I think she was trying to rescue me.

"Probably," I said. I had accompanied my mother to so many cities promoting her books that I just assumed I'd been to Richmond some time, but I couldn't think of any specific memory.

"Probably!" repeated Edwina. "What kind of answer is 'Probably'?"

" 'Probably' means he has no idea," answered Evans.

"No," said Dirk. " 'Probably' means Richmond is where Riley is."

"And he's been where Riley is before," added Evans.

"So, I should have said yes," I declared, noting to myself that my speech was fine. Had a couple of football players ripped me like this a year ago, it would have really rattled me. That's when I would have started mixing up letters or words. I have said, "Probabobaly," before, but I didn't this time.

"Do you know anything about Richmond?" asked Edwina.

All eyes turned to me.

After a moment of silence, Evans looked at Edwina and answered for me. "He knows that's where Riley is."

"I think it's sweet," said Cathy. That was her way of saying she had had enough football-player talk. If the past were any prediction about what would happen next, Dirk would take the hint, but Evans would not.

"When do you take off?" asked Harlan.

"That depends," I said. "I still have to arrange to have my records sent to . . . to. . . ." I realized that I didn't know where yet. Harlan was supposed to find out. Looking directly at her I jutted my face and raised my eyebrows in an effort to cue her help.

Before Evans and she had gotten so tight she would have responded right away, but she had gone to the dark side now. Feigning an innocent look, no easy task for Harlan, she rolled her fingers over, beckoning me to say more.

Evans laughed, "What's to . . . to? You're not going to dance school, are you?" Looking across the table at Dirk he added, "He doesn't have the legs for a tutu, does he?"

"Collegiate," answered Cathy for me as she took hold of Dirk's hand to ensure he didn't encourage Evans to continue.

"Collegiate?" I asked.

"That's where Riley told me she'd be going," answered Cathy.

I looked at Harlan, who confirmed the information with a nod of her head.

"Riley also said she'd be back for her senior year, so I assume you'll be back, too," said Cathy.

All eyes looked at me again.

"Of course he'll be back," declared Harlan before I could answer.

"Of course," I echoed.

"So, you're just going for the last month and a half of school," said Alice.

"I'm not sure," I said. And I wasn't. Until that moment I had only thought about being where Riley was. It hadn't dawned on me that I'd be gone. Gone from my family. Gone from my mom while she was sick. Gone from my home, my school, my friends. A wave of regret passed through me. I don't know if it was fear or sadness or guilt, but it felt like my temperature changed—first at my feet, then quickly through my body and out my head. I don't know what I must have looked like.

"You'll be okay," said Evans in a deeper voice.

CHAPTER 14

MR. GABRIEL'S QUESTION

"COLLEGIATE IS ONE OF THE PREMIER private schools in the country," said Mr. Gabriel when I told him the name of the school I'd be transferring to. "Have you visited it?"

"Not yet," I answered.

"Really?" He looked surprised. "But surely you've applied already. Yes?"

I hadn't even heard of Collegiate until lunchtime. I picked it because it was where Riley was going to go.

"Not really," I said. Hearing that it was one of the premier schools in the country made me second-guess whether I could get in or not. Until that moment I hadn't considered being turned down. I just assumed that private schools were schools you paid to go to, and since we could pay I never considered that it wouldn't work. Being told that I must apply opened up a whole new set of possibilities—all negative.

"Jasper," said Mr. Gabriel, using a tone that was designed to get my attention.

"Yes, sir," I said, refocusing on him.

"It looked like you drifted off there for a second, are you alright?"

"Yes sir."

He stood up from behind his desk and came around to sit on the edge of it. "Why don't you tell me what's going on?"

"Nothing." I knew it was a lame answer as soon as I said it. Of course there was something going on, and of course he was going to notice.

"Does this have anything to do with Riley transferring to Richmond?"

"No," I said, but immediately added, "Well, kinda."

"Look, Jasper. I've been on the phone with Mr. Lyons this morning. He and Riley are moving to Richmond, so her transfer is natural. Frankly, with a little more than a month to go before school is out for the summer I don't know if she'll get into Collegiate now either, but the chances of there being a second opening you could slide into are pretty slim. Your family isn't moving to Richmond, are they?"

"No."

"So you're following her."

We stared at each other. I was following her to Richmond, but that wasn't why I was leaving. It was just why I was going to Richmond. I was going because Aayma had told Carol to send me away. And until my mother was on her feet again, we had no choice but to do what Aayma said. I looked deeper into Mr. Gabriel's eyes. For some reason I wanted to tell him everything, but I realized what it would sound like.

Then I lied. "We need room on the farm, so I volunteered to go somewhere else." I shrugged. "Riley is why I picked Richmond, but do you think my family would let me just pack up and follow her?"

He leaned closer to me. "Your family?" he repeated.

I was confused, so tentatively I said, "Yeah, my family."

"That seems odd," he said more out loud than to me.

Straightening back up and folding his arms he added, "Is there something going on with your mom?"

I didn't see that question coming. It felt like a foot on my chest.

"Whad id you mean?" I fumbled my words out.

"You said your family wouldn't let you follow her."

I nodded.

"But it would have been more natural to say, 'My mother wouldn't let me follow her.'"

I had the feeling he had just caught me. I'm sure he had caught me, but other than the awkwardness of withholding information I had to withhold, he couldn't know what he had caught me at. I told myself it didn't matter.

"My mom wouldn't just let me follow Riley to Richmond," I explained, "but neither would my Aunt Maggie or my sister Carol."

He nodded slowly like he was thinking whether to say what he was thinking.

"What about the lab?" he finally asked.

"What about the lab?"

"The last time we talked you told me that research was your calling."

"Calling?" I repeated. I had no idea what he was talking about.

Holding up his hands in surrender he said, "Okay, that's my bad. The word 'calling' is my word. You didn't use that word."

"What does it mean?" I asked.

"It's sort of like your destiny or your vocation. It's what you were made for."

I nodded without looking directly at him. It's what I'd do when I wanted to disguise that I had no idea what some adult was talking about.

"If doing that lab work is your calling, Jasper, then you need to ask yourself how you are going to feel if you put it behind you."

"I'm just an ordinary kid," I defended.

He smiled and stared at me in a way that made me wonder if he could read my thoughts. Then he asked, "Do you know the story of David and Goliath?"

"Yes."

"He was just a kid, too."

CHAPTER 15

WALLY OBJECTS

"OF COURSE I OBJECT," said Wally. He was as close to mad as I had ever seen him. I can't hardly imagine him being outright mad. It isn't in his personality to be mad, especially with Carol, but he was frustrated. "There's something going on around here that isn't right."

We were all sitting around the dinner table. Maggie had made chili and served it with Fritos instead of with Carol's Irish beer bread, because with Fritos is the way I like it. It was my going-away-for-a-while dinner, and when that was explained to Wally he said, "What!" in as close to a yell as he ever had since I'd known him. Carol asked him if he objected, but I doubt she expected he'd say so if he did. But he did object, and he said so . . . and more.

Maggie stood up from the table. "I think I'll check on the patients."

"Me, too," I said, standing up.

Wally pointed his finger at my seat. "You're in this too, partner." When I sat back down, he looked back at Carol and snorted, "Carol, honey, I love you. You know I love you, but I can't keep overlooking what's going on around here. It isn't right."

There was a long silence while they just looked at each other, and I wished I was someplace else. Carol's first reaction was a gasp. I heard it. Then her eyebrows knit together, and she leaned toward him slightly. Wally's face didn't change. Then Carol's face slowly scrunched together, making her look confused at first, but then angry. She didn't stay angry long before biting her lower lip, which made Wally reach his hand out toward her. As soon as they were holding hands Carol sighed and said, "You're right."

He nodded his appreciation.

Carol looked at me, which surprised me. I took it to mean she wanted me to say something about telling Wally the truth, but I wasn't sure so I just said, "What?"

"He's part of our family," she said. "He should know about us."

It struck me funny, so I laughed, but that got me real dirty looks from both of them.

"This is serious, Jasper," said Carol.

"It is," added Wally. "There are two *serious* patients in this house, and this isn't a hospital. How long am I supposed to pretend that's okay?"

"I'm sorry," I told them. "I wasn't trying to make fun of you. It's just that when Carol said you should know about us, all I could think of was that *we* should know about us."

Carol, who was watching me, turned quickly to face Wally. "He's right. We're just finding out about us."

Wally rolled his eyes. "Come on, you two. This isn't a movie. I'm a scientist, for heaven's sake."

That's when Maggie strolled in, only it wasn't normal Maggie. It was black panther Maggie.

Wally was the first to see her come in. His eyes bugged out like in a cartoon. When I saw what he was looking at, I said, "I see you took your clothes off again."

CHAPTER 16

GOOD-BYE

I HAD ANOTHER NIGHT WITHOUT MUCH SLEEP. This time it was because I was thinking about driving to Richmond by myself, not to mention seeing Riley again. I had packed, showered, and shaved before going to bed. When I got up in the morning I got my things into my Cherokee and was sitting beside Mom's bed before anyone else was up.

Aunt Maggie was in Mom's room, too, but she was asleep on a chair in the corner. She woke up while I was wiping Mom's face with a cool damp cloth.

"You're up early, Jasper," observed Maggie from her chair.

I was glad she was awake because I had noticed something. Holding up the damp rag I asked, "Does it mean anything that Mom seems to be sweating quite a bit more today?" I was hoping it was a good sign because according to both Maggie and Wally the black mamba poison was expelled from the body through sweat.

Aunt Maggie yawned and stretched as she came to look over my shoulder.

"It is more sweat than usual, Jasper, but I think it is because we haven't been wiping her face so much while we slept," Maggie told me with a reassuring rub across my shoulders. "Don't worry. Her body is fighting the poison at her own speed."

Don't worry, I repeated to myself.

"Thank you for waiting to leave for Richmond," Maggie said, standing back up. "I'll send you off with a good breakfast. What would you like?"

"Bull's-eye eggs," I ordered right away, knowing what bread was still around. Maggie would cut a hole in a slice of bread and fry an egg in it. I especially loved it with Carol's Irish tea bread, so the choice was a no-brainer.

"Aunt Maggie," I asked, "you told me to wait to leave until after breakfast."

Waving her finger Maggie corrected me. "I asked you to wait. Not tell. Ask."

I don't remember the exact words she used, but I do remember that I didn't feel like I could refuse. "Is there something about the dark?" I asked.

As Aunt Maggie looked at me I could see her lips begin to form a word. She was going to speak, I'm sure of it, but then she didn't. As she left she muttered, "Just be safe, boy."

That's why I'm being sent to Richmond. That's what I thought.

Alone again with Mom I did the best I could to keep her cool and cleaned up. I laid my head on the pillow next to hers, with my face looking into the side of her head. I didn't realize why I did it until I noticed myself rooting around a little for a better sniff of her hair. My mother's hair always smelled like honeysuckle to me, so when I was little and feeling scared I'd bury my head in the nape of her neck. Smelling that honeysuckle always meant everything was okay.

There was no comfort to be found this time. The honeysuckle smell was there, but it was weak. What was there this time was the smell of her drool soaked into her pillow. It was not a pleasant smell, but it wasn't supposed to be either.

I wolfed my breakfast down, thinking the sooner I was done, the sooner I could hit the road. I was still chewing about a quarter of my third bull's-eye egg when I took my plate to the sink.

"Slow down, Jasper," Aunt Maggie told me. "Go sit with the big man while I make breakfast for your sister. Richmond will be there when you get there."

I went to Oberon's room, but I wasn't thrilled about it. It took me awhile to agree to go, but once I did, I didn't want to wait.

Oberon was sleeping on his back, just like Mom, but he was sweating more. Mom's drooling had soaked her pillow to the point that we'd have to throw it away when this was all over. With Oberon we were going to have to throw away the mattress. I wiped his face and chest with a cool damp rag and then went back to the kitchen.

"What are you doing now?" asked Carol when I entered.

She had caught me smelling my fingers. Oberon's toxin smell was similar to Mom's, but quite a bit stronger. I wondered if it was going to come off my hands.

Holding my fingers out to Carol I said, "Smell."

"I'm not doing that," she snarled. "What are you, ten?"

"It's the toxin smell," I told her. "Oberon's spit smells just like Mom's."

She shook her head and hugged me, saying, "You and your nose." Then she squeezed me tighter and added, "Thank you for agreeing to go. We'll take care of Mom. You take care of yourself." Then she let go of me and said, "I left a bag of stuff for you on your front seat. Now, go on."

CHAPTER 17

RICHMOND: TUESDAY

IT TOOK ME SIX AND A HALF HOURS to drive from Boone to Richmond, the longest trip I'd ever taken by myself. It seemed to take a lot longer than six and a half hours while I was driving, but once I got to Richmond it felt like it had gone quickly. I had listened to, or should I say I played, an audio book of *Watership Down*. Carol had given it to me when I left that morning. She also gave me a bag of vegan chocolate chip cookies, two apples, three bottles of water, and a handful of twenty-dollar bills.

"Wally stills thinks this is the wrong thing to do," Carol had told me through the open window of my car. I could see the strain on her forehead as she asked, "You think we're doing the right thing, don't you?"

"I do," I said, but I didn't know. As I approached Richmond, the thought that I had left my mother haunted me more and more. Maggie said my leaving was the right thing to do, and Maggie always knew the right thing to do. "We have to give your mother time to heal," she had said. I believed that.

As I parked in front of Riley's father's house I still believed we were doing the right thing, but the last thought I had before getting out of the car was what Wally had said: "Time may be a great healer, but you and I are in the healing business, too, Jasper."

Although Aunt Maggie had said she knew someone I could stay with, I arranged to stay with Riley's father, King Lyons. I knew him, and at least as far as I could tell, he liked me, so I preferred that to staying with a stranger. I also knew that he was living alone while Riley was staying with her aunt. That way she could have a stable place to stay while she finished the school year, and he could come and go whenever business opportunities came up.

"You found it okay," said Mr. Lyons from the front step of the house as I got out of my car. He had asked that I call him and let him know when I was just outside of Richmond, so he was watching for me when I got there.

"GPS," I explained.

"I figured," he said, walking toward me. "In my day we didn't have things like GPS to get us anywhere. Can I help you with some bags?"

I had brought one large suitcase full of clothes and a small suitcase full of other stuff. I also had Mom's credit card if I needed to buy anything else. Mr. Lyons hauled my big suitcase up the stairs to my room while I dragged the smaller one. My bag was heavier because it held all my electronic stuff. The quick tour ended in the kitchen. He fixed himself a cup of coffee and me a glass of lemonade as we settled in around the kitchen table.

"Thank you for letting me stay with you," I said.

"Not a problem," he said, but with a scowl, "not a problem at all." His scowl stayed as he stared at his coffee cup. "I'm glad you're here. I'm worried about Riley. I've got her an appointment with a counselor here in Richmond for next week. She talked to a woman named Elizabeth Abel in Boone a couple of times before we left. She said Riley was doing as well as to be expected, but she gave us the name of a woman here in Richmond and strongly suggested we continue." He looked up at me and said, "I was encouraged by that, but then the first day we were here she had a panic attack." He shook his head slowly and looked back down, "It was bad."

"What happened?" I had talked to Riley on the phone most days since they left for Richmond, but she never mentioned anything like this.

"She had gone for a walk at a park her aunt told her about. We thought it would be good for her, you know, outside, fresh air, a petting zoo. But that's what did it. She got near the birds over there and had what we thought was a heart attack. They called an ambulance and took her to the ER. That's where they told us it was a panic attack." Looking back up at me again, "I just never imagined anything would threaten us like this."

I waited and watched until he said, "You were threatened, too, weren't you?"

I knew the answer right away, of course, but it took me a moment to nod yes.

"And is your family threatened, too?"

I didn't answer that right away either, but he didn't wait. "Of course they were. You wouldn't be here otherwise."

"No, sir."

He made a fist. "I just wish I knew who these people were. I'd hire mercenaries and rid the world of them."

"Yes, sir," I said. It felt very weird hearing him talk like that.

His face softened as he shook his head, "I'm sorry. I'm just blowing off steam. I've been in cutthroat competition in business before, but threatening my daughter. . . ." He shook his head again without finishing his sentence. "I don't know, Jasper. I just don't know."

I wanted to tell him that as soon as my mom got better she'd usher forces of nature that would make his mercenaries look like Cub Scouts, but I didn't. Why would he believe me?

"What's Dr. Beery going to do?"

"Wally was almost finished setting up his lab at our farm this weekend, but now he's supposed to take it apart. He didn't want to, but he said he would." I took my first sip of the lemonade. It was the kind you make with a powder. It either had too much water or too little powder. "Wally didn't want me to leave Boone either."

"No?"

"No," I answered.

"I suppose he didn't approve of my leaving either, did he?"

"No, sir," I told him. "But he didn't say anything bad."

Mr. Lyons chuckled twice. "No. He wouldn't say anything bad. But he and I look at some things very differently."

I had no idea what he was talking about, so I was glad he continued.

"You see, for me the lab was a business. It was how I made a living. It was how I took care of Riley. You understand that, don't you?"

I nodded yes.

"But for Wally, it's who he is." He sat back. "I admire that in him. I'm actually a little jealous of him for that, but it's a trap."

"He's trapped?" I asked.

"For me it's a business. When it's profitable I ride it out, but when it's not profitable, I move on." When he said, "move on," he gestured with his thumb toward the door. "But Wally, he can't just move on. It's who he is. He can't get away from that."

"He doesn't want to," I added.

"No," agreed Mr. Lyons. "That's part of the trap."

CHAPTER 18

RILEY RETURNS

"WHAT'S PART OF THE TRAP?" It was Riley. She was standing in the kitchen doorway. Her tone was crisp and her face knit together in a serious expression that was nowhere close to the surprised, glad-to-see-you reaction I had looked forward to ever since I got permission to come.

"Hi, honey," greeted Riley's dad. "Look who's here."

She glanced at me. She still looked cross. "Were you talking about me?"

Mr. Lyons and I looked at each other. I was hoping he knew what she was talking about. It looked like he had the same idea about me.

"We were talking about Dr. Beery, Jasper's brother-in-law," he explained. "Why did you think we were talking about you?"

Riley's rigid posture went limp. I thought she was going to collapse, but she didn't. She did cry a little as she said, "I just don't want anyone to be trapped by me."

I didn't know what to do. If I had been alone with her I would have put my arms around her, but with her father sitting next to me it didn't seem right. He did what I wanted to do, and as soon as he pulled her head toward his chest she started to cry.

Between her crying and how her face was buried in her father's chest I could barely understand her when she said, "You sold your business and left Boone," then in a louder voice she added, "because of me." She cried even harder then.

He waited until she calmed down enough to hear him and said, "Honey, none of that was because of you. You were put in danger because of that business."

"But if I hadn't been there to threaten," she tried to explain.

"If you hadn't been there, they would have found another way to come after me. It's not your fault." He held her away from him so that he could see her face. "Do you hear me? It's not your fault."

Her eyes were red, but she wasn't crying. She looked at me and said, "And now Jasper had to leave Boone, too."

"How did you know that?" asked her dad.

Riley forced a smile and a shrug.

"Did you read my email?" asked her dad.

"Maybe," she said weakly.

Mr. Lyons looked at me and chuckled. "So much for that surprise." To Riley he said, "Jasper isn't trapped either. He had to leave Boone, but he could have gone anywhere. He chose Richmond." Looking at me again he asked, "You chose Richmond, right, son?"

I nodded yes.

He looked back at Riley. "Jasper missed *me,*" he told her and then flinched as if she was going to slug him. The slug never came, though. I'm pretty sure she wasn't in the mood for joking.

She looked around him as he hugged her again and mouthed, "I'm sorry," at me.

Riley's dad kept his left arm around her but swung his body around so that he was facing me. "Why don't you take Jasper to see the birds, and when you get back I'll take us out to the

Egg & I for dinner." I found out that later that the Egg & I is a restaurant that serves breakfast foods, which I love.

"I'll drive," I volunteered, standing up.

Riley nodded yes and held her left hand out to me.

"Take your time," said her dad as we walked out to my Cherokee.

We were quiet as we walked to the car, as I opened the door for her, and even when I closed it. It wasn't until I sat behind the wheel that she actually spoke directly to me.

"I'm sorry," she said.

"Why are you sorry?"

"I don't believe you came here because you were threatened," she said, looking hard at me.

"It's true," I said immediately.

She frowned. I don't think she believed me.

"Really, really," I said. I shook my head once to reboot my brain. "I meant, 'Really, Riley.' Whoever forced your dad to sell Lion Pharmaceuticals doesn't want Wally and me to run a lab either."

She watched me as I spoke.

"Really," I tried again. "I just had to get out of town until Wally packs up the lab."

"Is that what he's doing now?"

"I don't know," I said. I thought about telling her he was, but I figured if I lied to her it would be worse when she found out the truth. "Carol wants him to tear it down, but he doesn't want to. I guess they're still working it out."

"What does your mom say?" she asked.

It was the right question, but I wasn't prepared for it.

"She's not saying anything," I said. It was kinda true.

"She's letting them decide," suggested Riley.

"What's with the birds?" I asked, changing the subject.

She rolled her eyes and slid around to buckle her seat belt. "Didn't my dad tell you about my panic attack?"

I buckled in and started the car as I said, "He told me you started seeing a counselor here after you started having nightmares."

She directed me as I drove. "The nightmares started after I had a meltdown at the children's petting zoo at Maymont. There were a couple of turkey buzzards that came near me, and I just keeled over."

"What are you dreaming about?" I asked.

"I don't know. I don't remember the dreams at all. I just wake up and my heart is beating fast and I'm all sweaty." She looked at me while we were stopped at a traffic light. "That was a panic attack you had, wasn't it?"

"Yeah."

"Did you have nightmares afterward?"

"I didn't, but I think that's because Wally knew exactly what caused it."

She nodded. "I remember. It was too many strong smells all at once."

"Do you know what caused yours?"

Shaking her head no, she said, "My counselor says that my avoidance of the bird area is a hint at what caused it, but he says we can't be sure unless the memories come back."

"What about . . . you know . . . ?" I stumbled.

"Hendersonville," she finished for me. "That's what we talk about mostly, but how that's connected to the birds is a mystery."

It wasn't a mystery to me. I knew exactly what the connection was between her abduction and captivity in Hendersonville and the turkey buzzards. I wanted to tell her I knew. I wanted to tell her everything I knew, but I couldn't do that.

"So why are we going there now?"

"It's part of my therapy. Instead of avoiding that place I go there every day. So far I don't go to the petting zoo, but each day I get a little closer. Usually I just walk around and look at the gardens and the people playing Frisbee golf. There's even a big bear habitat. That's my favorite spot. Do you want to go see the bears?"

"Sure."

"Eventually," she continued, "I'll go right over to the turkey buzzards and feed them."

I didn't think I was supposed to respond to that until she asked, "Do you believe me?"

"Of course I do. I believe you can do anything you want to do."

She smiled, then put her hand gently on my right forearm. For the first time since I got to Richmond she looked like Riley.

CHAPTER 19

MAYMONT

RILEY TOOK ME TO MAYMONT, the park where she had her panic attack. It's a 100-acre park that was once a private estate. The Victorian mansion is now a museum, and it is surrounded by gardens, walking and running paths, nature exhibits, and the petting zoo where Riley had her panic attack.

We held hands and walked slowly by the petting zoo. Riley didn't seem nervous to me as we passed by, but she didn't glance in that direction either. There were definitely turkey buzzards in there. I could smell them.

"Will you start Collegiate tomorrow?" she asked.

She pulled her head back as she looked at me.

"I thought about it, but Mr. Gabriel talked me out of transferring. Are you disappointed?"

"I am. And I think you will be, too. Collegiate is pretty awesome. This is their 100th anniversary. Did you know that Russell Wilson went to Collegiate?"

"I did," I said. "Do you know who Russell Wilson is?"

"Of course," she bragged. "He just won the Super Bowl." She punched me lightly on the right arm. "We watched it together. Remember?"

"But did you know who he is before you came here?"

"No," she confessed, rubbing my arm apologetically.

"Me either," I told her, "but Dirk and Evans sure know who he is."

"So the Adversity table knows you're here."

"They do. I had Harlan contact you Monday morning to find out what school you were at, so of course, by lunchtime they all knew."

"Of course," she laughed once. "I miss them."

"I know," I said.

"I read your email to Dad Sunday night, so I knew you were coming. Then when Harlan asked about Collegiate I just assumed you'd be transferring, too."

"I would have, but since I'm going to go back to Watauga for my senior year it makes more sense to finish this year with online classes from Watauga."

"I didn't know you could do that," she said, sounding disappointed. "That's what I should have done."

"Where you go to school right now doesn't matter so much, but we all hope you'll be back for your senior year, too."

Riley smiled one of those courtesy smiles, so I knew she didn't have much hope that it would work out that way. "That would be nice," she said weakly. "You have a home to go back to, and as soon as that lab is torn apart your family will let you return. But I don't know what it will take for us to return. Dad's already sold his business, and he's looking into other things now." She squeezed my hand. "It doesn't look good."

We stopped walking. The bear habitat was just off the sidewalk to our left.

"What is it?" asked Riley, looking at me.

I was picking up a smell that was intriguing me. I think I must have looked like a dog sticking my nose up like an antenna. "I smell something," I explained. Looking toward the bear habitat

I said, "I think it's that way." I looked at Riley, and with only my eyes I pleaded with her to let me go.

Somehow she knew what I wanted. She nodded her permission.

I got to the edge of the bear habitat and scanned for the bears. I knew that what I was smelling was a mammal. I guessed that it was the bears. When I spotted them I pointed at them. They were directly across from where I stood. I pointed to let Riley know that's where I was headed although I didn't look to see if she noticed before I began sprinting around the enclosure for a better whiff.

When I got to the other side I could no longer see them, but I knew they were right under me because the smell was so strong.

I don't know what I must have looked like standing there taking in deep breaths with my eyes closed. I don't know if anyone was looking or how long I was standing there with a dippy look of satisfaction on my face.

"You look like you just walked into a bakery," said Riley, standing next to me.

"Doesn't that smell great?" I blurted.

She frowned, "It smells like a barn, Jasper."

I laughed. "I didn't mean it smelled good. I mean I just figured something out."

"What?" she asked.

I looked at her and realized that I couldn't tell her what I wanted to tell her. *Oberon's a bear,* I pictured myself saying, but I knew I couldn't. "Wally has something at the lab that he can't identify and I just figured out what it is."

"It's a black bear?" said Riley.

"It's not a black bear, but it's some kind of a bear."

"That's wonderful," she said.

I think she meant it, too. She had no idea why it was important or how it mattered. All she knew was that I figured it out and I was delighted and that was all she needed to know to know it was wonderful. That was wonderful.

"I have to text Wally," I told her.

"So text him," she said, sliding her left hand under my right elbow. She began leading me back toward the car while I typed in my message.

I texted, "OBERON IS A BEAR."

I knew I might not get a response right away because Wally didn't keep close tabs on his phone. But I did get a quick response. We were halfway back to the car when my phone vibrated. It was Wally.

"Hi, Wally," I said into the phone.

"You gotta come back, Jasper."

"What?"

"I think I can get an antidote for your mom, but I need your help."

"I . . . ah . . . just got here," I stammered.

My comment alarmed Riley enough for her to stop walking, drop her hand from my arm, and stare at me with her eyebrows bunched together.

"It's Wally," I told Riley. "He wants me to go back to Boone."

"Riley's listening," said Wally.

"Yes," I told him.

"No problem," he continued. "Maggie says you can't travel at night, but you have to come back tomorrow. Call me later when you can talk."

"Okay," I said. Before I turned my phone off, I asked, "Did you see my text?" but he was already gone.

"You're going back to Boone," said Riley.

"I don't know yet," I said.

"I do," she said, slipping her hand back under my arm.

CHAPTER 20

THE EGG & I

ON THE WAY HOME WE DROVE BY COLLEGIATE. It stretched across a huge block, looking more like a college campus than any high school I had ever seen. It was nearly 6:30 when we got back to Riley's father's house. He was standing on the front steps when we drove up.

"Let's go to dinner," he said as we climbed out of my car.

"Jasper's going home tomorrow," announced Riley.

"You're leaving tomorrow?" asked King.

"I don't know yet," I said.

"Yes," said Riley.

"Wally's working on an antidote, and he thinks I can help," I explained.

"He knows you can help," corrected Riley.

I looked at her. "Do you want me to go?"

"Of course."

That struck me like a punch in the stomach.

I must have looked pitiful. Riley put her right hand on my left forearm and looked at her father until he went back inside. Then she turned to me and said, "It's not that I really want you to go. I just want you to do what's right for you, and that's to go. They need you, Jasper. The only reason you're here is because of me and that's a reason to visit. It's not a reason to stay. You have to go home, Jasper."

"I know," I said.

"Good," she said as she leaned toward me and kissed my cheek.

I started to put my arms around her, but that's when the door opened and her dad came back out.

"Hungry?" he asked.

The Egg & I restaurant was about twenty-five minutes away. While we drove, King told me all about historical Richmond, the slave auctions, the Civil War, and the visit from Abraham Lincoln. "The church where Patrick Henry said, 'Give me liberty or give me death,' is just over there," King pointed as we drove by.

At the restaurant, King ordered a New Orleans Benedict with Andouille sausage and tomato gravy. Riley ordered a Veggie Benedict with portobello mushrooms and Greek seasoning. For me it was a toss-up between the Mexican skillet and the Mexican omelet. I chose the skillet because the waitress said it was more food. I excused myself. Once I was alone in the bathroom I closed myself in a stall and called Wally.

"Can we talk?" he asked, answering his phone.

"We're at a restaurant," I told him. "I'm in the bathroom so I can't talk long. What's up?"

"Do you know what detoxification is?"

"No."

"It's the process where your body gets rid of toxins through sweat and saliva. That's why your mom is drooling so much. Her body is fighting off the poison."

"Aunt Maggie told us that, too. So it's scientific, huh?"

"It is."

"So that's good, right?" I said.

"Yes. And the same thing is happening with Oberon."

"Was he bit by the same thing?"

"Actually, Jasper, I was hoping you could tell me."

I didn't know how to respond.

He continued, "Does his sweat smell like hers?"

I thought. "Maybe," I said tentatively.

"You don't sound sure."

"I'm not," I said. "I'm sorry."

"Carol thought you had said something like that before you left this morning."

"That's right. I did say that," I remembered.

"There was a lot going on and you weren't looking for that sort of connection, but that's why I need you home. If Oberon's struggling with the same thing, then he's developing antibodies to fight it off. I don't know how compatible bears and humans are, but we just might be able to use Oberon's blood to develop antibodies for your mother."

It was the first hopeful thing I'd heard in a while. Forgetting Aayma's threat I said, "I'll drive back tonight."

"No, Jasper," said Wally. "Get a good night's sleep and drive home tomorrow. We've talked about it here, and Maggie says that you must wait until the morning to return. She was absolutely insistent about that."

"Is Carol okay with me coming back?" I asked.

"Carol has agreed, but she isn't comfortable. But seriously, Jasper, Maggie says I have to get you to swear that you won't return until in the morning."

"I swear," I said, "I won't return until in the morning."

CHAPTER 21

BYRON

I TURNED OFF MY PHONE AND STEPPED OUT from the stall only to find that I hadn't been as alone as I had thought. There, leaning against the wall across from the stall was a guy watching me. He had on baggy shorts, hiking boots, and a brown Piggly Wiggly T-shirt. His short hair was dyed blue, his ears were pierced with studs, and in his mouth was a red Tootsie Pop.

"I'm sorry," I said, assuming he had been waiting to use the facility.

"I hope not," he mumbled around the sucker.

The comment alarmed me and I stepped back, which probably wasn't the smartest defensive maneuver I could have tried.

"You're not being very careful, Jasper," he said in a Kentucky accent.

I knew that his knowing my name was either very, very good or very, very bad, I just didn't know which.

"Whad da do wand?" I asked.

He snorted once through his nose and stood up away from the wall. "What I want is for you to be more careful." He held out his hand. "I'm just a country boy, but I just followed you in here and you didn't notice."

I shook his hand. It was small but strong.

"How do you know my name?" I asked.

He grinned. Taking out the sucker he said, "Oh, I know who you are. The better question is why don't you know who I am?"

That confused me.

"No, we haven't met, if that's what you're thinking." With the Tootsie Pop he gestured at my nose and added, "But you should recognize me with that."

With that I became more aware of my sense of smell, realizing I did recognize his odor. I just couldn't place it.

"My name is Byron. Byron Mary."

"Rose," I blurted, pointing at him.

He grinned. "There you go, buddy. Rose is my sister."

"You're a . . ."—I stopped because I didn't know what was okay to say and what wasn't.

Byron laughed. "I'm a wolverine and proud of it."

"Are you following me?" I asked.

"Not you, Jasper. We're here keeping an eye on your girl-friend. But there's been nothing to watch until you got here."

I stepped back again.

"There's two vultures following you, Jasper. So far they've stayed pretty far away, but they're watching."

I looked toward the door as if I could see them.

"They're not here," he said. "They're vultures. They can only transition in the night."

Although I'd seen other change back and forth in the daylight his confused me. Here he was in human form, and it was still day-light. I pointed at him.

"Me," he said. "I'm no filthy buzzard. I am a servant of the Mother. While we are in her service we have the power to transi-tion whenever it is right."

"I'm going back to Boone," I told him.

"That will make Richmond safer for Riley, but you need to watch for those birds."

©

I returned to the table and tried to make sure I didn't alert either Riley or her father to the presence of Byron Mary on the other side of the room. I suppose I managed it because neither of them ever glanced in his direction. But I glanced in his direction several times, and always with the same result. Whenever he caught me looking, and he always did, he'd point at his own eyes with two fingers and shake his head no.

When we left the restaurant parking lot, neither Riley nor her father noticed the cream-colored Mini Cooper that pulled out from the curb as we passed. Byron Mary wasn't in that car as it followed us to the highway, but the male driver and the female passenger bore a striking resemblance to the Marys. They were both on the small side of average in stature, and they both had short hair dyed to bright colors. The driver's was green, and the passenger's was pink. They were hardly what I'd call inconspicuous. I was glad Riley had the wolverines watching out for her, but that it was needed concerned me a great deal.

"What's wrong?" whispered Riley as she took hold of my hand. She asked softly enough to keep her father from hearing as he listened to a Pandora jazz station.

We were sitting in the backseat of his Lincoln Town Car to have some of what he called "alone time." I won't say that his looking at us in the rearview mirror every few seconds bothered me, but it sure didn't feel like alone time either. "I'm okay," I said, timing my response to just after one of his glances.

Leaning against me she said, "You have to go home, Jasper."

I started to say I knew, but she put her finger against my lips

93

and said, "We'll be fine. I promise. If we spend our senior years apart, we'll be back together the year after."

King glanced at Riley leaning toward me, and I think he grinned. I could only see his eyes in the mirror, but I think his cheek bulged out and his ear went up. I was glad. I was also glad that I wasn't leaning back. Maybe that's why he grinned.

She took her finger away. "Nothing about us can be right if you aren't true to yourself, and that means going home."

"I know."

"Good," she said, laying her head on my shoulder.

We rode the rest of the way to her aunt's house with her holding my left arm and resting her head on my shoulder. I walked her to the door feeling weighted down by the desire to cry and the slightly larger need not to.

At the door she turned to face me and said, "You have to do what you're supposed to do."

She didn't wait for me to respond. She just looked at her father sitting in his car and circled her finger around until he faced the other way. Then she kissed me and went inside.

I don't know how long I stood there looking at the closed door, but I didn't move until I heard King Lyons call out from the car, "It's time, partner."

CHAPTER 22

ANOTHER FLIGHT TO BOONE

I WOKE UP AT 3:30 THE NEXT MORNING with her last words running laps through my head. "You gotta do what you gotta do."

I knew I had to go back. I knew I had to help Wally find an antidote for Mom. I knew he thought I could do it, and I knew Riley and her dad thought I could do it, but from the moment I knew I was going back to Boone the thought that I might not be able to do it started growing. I'd never been the last resort before, and it was scaring me more than I'd ever been scared before, and that was saying something. In the past year I'd been threatened by Dobermans, wolves, snakes, and buzzards, and oh yeah, a murderer tried to kill me once and kidnap me another time. But having my mother's fate in my hands was the scariest by far. As I lie there thinking about how odd my fears were, I realized that I wouldn't be going back to sleep, so I got up.

Getting ready to leave was pretty simple since I hadn't unpacked. I stopped at a WaWa gas station on the way out of town and got myself a breakfast sandwich and a large hot cocoa, which was way too hot to drink. It was dark, and the traffic on the outskirts of Richmond was too busy for me to try to manage the heat of the drink or the sandwich that was wrapped up like a Christmas present.

Once I was well out of town and beyond the traffic I pulled over on the shoulder of the road to organize my breakfast. The first thing I did was get out of the car to unwrap my sandwich. I was afraid to stay in the car and try to tear the paper wrapper open because the last thing I wanted to do was sit in runny scrambled eggs and melted cheese all the way back to Boone. I managed to get it open without losing any of the contents, so I set it on the hood to cool while I leaned in for the hot cocoa. As I stood there concentrating on getting the lid off so that it would be cool enough to enjoy, I didn't see that something that was about to land on the roof of my Jeep Cherokee.

CRASH!

The sound was deafening, and it was also just a few feet from my head. I must have jumped backward because I distinctly remember flying away from the contents of my cup, which was flying faster toward me than I was falling away.

"Ahhhhh!" I screamed as the hot liquid spread across my chest.

From the flat of my back I pulled my T-shirt away from my chest and ventured a look at whatever it was that hit my car.

"Rahhhahaha," screeched the ugliest and largest vulture I had ever seen. It was perched on the edge of my roof as it hunched over staring at me with its beady eyes.

I didn't move. I was too scared to move. But I knew I couldn't just lie there either. After remaining still for what felt like minutes I decided to try to get up. I hoped that if I could stand slowly enough, I might be able to dive into my front seat and get the door closed before the vulture reacted.

By the time I got to my feet the vulture had slid down the roof to just above the still-open driver's door. I didn't dare try to dive in with the ugly brute so close, so I decided to try something else. His eyes followed me as I sidestepped my way around the door.

He watched as I picked up the sandwich and waved it back and forth. He kept watching as I threw it over the car and into the ditch. He watched, but he didn't move, and his eyes only lost contact with mine for a tiny second.

"*Rahhhahaha,*" screeched the vulture again, this time leaning even farther forward.

I could smell his breath this time. I had smelled it before. It was just as foul as I remembered.

"*RAHHHAHAHA!*" it screeched with three times the volume.

I don't know if it was his breath or his volume, but something forced me backward, and again I found myself on my back. I rolled over as fast as I could and scrambled to my knees. Before I could get to my feet, another vulture thudded down right in front of me. I know it was another because the one behind me dropped down from the roof of my car and landed on the middle of my back. The impact knocked the wind out of me.

Lying there flattened and pinned down, I remembered that the last time I'd seen these brutes there was a poisonous snake with them. The thought of that snake, the one that killed Detective Ward and bit my mother, sent an energizing wave of panic through me. I began to roll and thrash, trying to get the vulture off my back.

My efforts got me another deafening screech from the one on my back. It was right on the side of my head. I thought my ear would implode. I turned my head away from the noise and buried my face in my arms. My right ear was tucked against my shoulder, and I covered the left with my left hand. Protecting my ears was all I could think to do.

"*RAYYYAYAYA! Rayyyayaya!*"

Even with my ears covered I could tell that this sounded different. I could feel the weight of the vulture on my back suddenly being removed. I could tell by the sound that the second cry was farther from me than the first. The vultures were gone. It took me a minute to look around, but they were gone and there was no sign of why they were gone. It was like they suddenly just disappeared.

I wondered if any of it had really happened, but only for a moment. My sandwich was in a ditch and my hot cocoa was all over my chest, attracting that gray gravel dust that's all over the sides of roads. Also, my right ear still felt like it was full of water.

A car slowed down as it approached. I wanted help or at least to know that there were other human beings around, but I didn't want to have to explain why I looked like I did. I managed to be standing as they drove by. There were two guys in the car. They looked to be my age or a little older. The one in the passenger seat pointed at me and laughed. "Party hard," he said as they sped on.

"Party hard," I chuckled. At least I didn't have to explain.

I surveyed the area. There was still no sign of the vultures. It was dark, but there was a glimmer of the breaking of day to the east.

I stood there until my phone rang.

"Jasper," said Carol in a hurried voice.

"Carol."

"I'm sorry to call now, Jasper. I know I woke you up, but I had to call."

She sounded shook up, which worried me. "It's okay, Carol. Is Mom okay?" I asked.

"Oh, yeah. I mean, she's not really okay, but she's the same." She sighed into the phone. "This is embarrassing, I know. I just had another nightmare, but it was about you. I know it's silly, but I needed to hear your voice."

"It's okay. I was already up."

"Well, remember that Maggie told you to wait until daylight to start back."

"I remember," I said, but I didn't tell her that my memory hadn't retrieved that until she just mentioned it. Changing the subject I asked, "So, tell me, what happened in your nightmare?"

"It's weird. I felt like I was watching you from very high and very far away, but I could see you very clearly. Anyway, you were standing next to your car when this giant bird landed on it." She then said as if she was shuddering, "I hate birds. Then you threw coffee all over yourself and fell down. The next thing that happened is you were face down and the bird was on top of you."

She paused. "Are you still there?"

"Yeah," I said, but I wasn't sure where I was or what was real.

"Crazy, huh?"

Not as crazy as me, I thought. "What happened next?"

"In my dream?"

"Yeah."

"I don't know," she said. "I had the feeling of falling out of the sky. My nightmares often end like that. That's when I wake up."

"Carol," I said softly.

"Yes."

"I'm glad you called." It was true. I was glad she called. I wasn't sure what to do with what I just heard, but I was sure it was important. *Mom would know,* was my next thought.

"Thanks, Jasper. See you later."

"Later," I agreed.

I sat back in my car and locked the doors, but I didn't start it until the sun was fully in view.

CHAPTER 23

THE MOTHER WOULD KNOW

THE DRIVE BACK TO BOONE was painfully slow. I'd catch myself driving slower and slower, waiting and watching for the vultures to return. When that happened I'd tell myself to speed up, which would work until I'd start thinking about Carol's nightmare. Thinking about that would slow me down again until I'd notice and speed up again. It was nearly three o'clock when I finally made it home.

I'd only been gone overnight, but I was surprised that the place looked the same to me. The only greeting I got was from Kitty, who was tending to the alpacas in the back pasture. Kitty barked, and I waved.

I headed straight to Mom's room, hoping that if someone was with her, it would be Maggie and not Carol. I wanted to talk about the one thing I couldn't talk to Carol about: Carol.

Maggie was there, tucking the corner of a sheet under Mom's bed when I walked in. Her chanting kept her from hearing me right away. "Baby," she said when she finally looked up and noticed me. "Baby" was what she called me when I was little and would run into her arms. I hadn't run into her arms in years, but I was tempted right then.

"Mr. Carol wanted to see you as soon as you got here," Maggie told me. "Mr. Carol" was what she called Wally when he couldn't hear. I think he knew anyway.

"I need to talk to you first," I told her.

She nodded and pointed at the chair on the other side of Mom's bed. "You talk. I work." With that she went back to finishing making Mom's bed.

"How is she?" I asked as I sat down.

"She is the same, but the big man is improving. Mr. Carol thinks he can use the big man's blood to help the Mother." Looking directly at me she added, "He needs your help with that. That is why he is in a hurry to see you."

"I know," I said. "Something happened to me on the way home that I want to tell you about. I don't know if it's important or not, but it feels important."

Maggie's face grew more serious. She tucked Mom's blanket over her and then came around the bed and sat across from me. "Speak to me."

"I didn't exactly wait until daylight to leave Richmond."

Maggie stood up immediately, bearing her lower teeth. "What happened?" she demanded.

"I was attacked by a couple of vultures."

"For heaven's sake!" she said as she lifted me out of my seat by my arms. Half smelling and half looking, she began to examine my neck and head for wounds.

"I'm fine," I said firmly. "They didn't touch me."

She let me go and stepped back to look in my eyes. I had seen that look before. She was deciding if I was telling the truth or not.

"I was standing outside of my car when one of them landed on the roof. I tried to distract it by throwing my sandwich."

Maggie's piercing stare and knotted forehead didn't change.

"That would have worked if it had just been a regular old vulture," I explained.

Maggie was unimpressed. "Go on."

"The rest is confusing. Another one came, and I ended up on my stomach with one of them on my back."

"Take off your shirt," she ordered.

"I'm fine," I told her again.

She frowned. "How could that be?"

"I don't know. I really don't. Something came and took the one off my back. I'm sorry. I was too scared to look."

"But you are unhurt?"

"Yes," I said.

"Thank heaven," she said and began to return to making Mom's bed.

"Wait," I blurted. "That's not the weird part."

The frown returned to Maggie's face as she slowly turned to face me again. "Yes."

"Right after it all happened, Carol called me. She said she had had a dream about me and wanted to check on me."

"She had a premonition," explained Maggie.

"No," I said, shaking my head. "It wasn't a premonition. She told me everything that happened. She described where I was. She described how I spilled my cocoa, threw my sandwich, and fell over." Shaking my head I said, "Maggie, I know it's impossible, but I think she was there. She saw it all happen, and I think she saved me."

Maggie's eyes drifted up and away from me. She seemed lost in her own thoughts.

Finally I asked, "What does it mean?"

Maggie looked back at me. "I do not know, but the Mother would know. That is why you should go find Wally."

She was still looking toward the ceiling as I stood to go. Before I got to the door she said, "I am glad you are here and safe, but you must do what I tell you to do from now on. Do you understand?"

"Are you talking about me not waiting for daylight?"

"I am. Do you believe me now?"

"I do," I said. "But what's the deal about the dark?"

"It was only a suspicion, but now it is confirmed," she said.

"What is confirmed?"

"Not now," she answered firmly. "You have responsibilities to tend to now." Her tone did not leave room for debate.

CHAPTER 24

A QUEST FOR JASPER

WALLY AND CAROL WERE WAITING for me in the kitchen.

Carol ran over and threw her arms around me when I walked in. "I'm glad you're safe, but I still don't want you here."

"I know," I said.

Carol let go of me. Turning to face Wally she said, "I hope you and Maggie are right. I really do."

"We voted to bring you back," explained Wally. "I argued that we need your help, and she argued that they would leave us be if you were gone."

"And he convinced Aunt Maggie," snapped Carol.

"I didn't trick her into agreeing with me, Carol. I stated my case, you stated yours, and Maggie found my argument more convincing."

Carol's eyes flashed. She looked back at me and said, "That dream I had this morning felt so real. I just needed to hug you to be sure you are okay." She hugged me again. This time it was tighter and a bit more uncomfortable.

"Carol's been having disturbing dreams for a while," Wally explained.

She relaxed her grip around my neck and said, "He thinks I need an antidepressant."

"It'll help with the anxiety," he said.

Carol snorted, "My anxiety is *not* in my head. It's real. Aayma is real. You didn't see her. I saw her. She's serious. Look what she's done already."

"Those things *are* real," said Wally. "But you know what I'm talking about."

Carol took a step back. "A lot of my dreams include me falling from very high places. Mr. Science over there thinks I have a fear of heights that a pill can fix."

"There's something going on with you, and I want you to get help."

Carol let go of me and headed toward the kitchen door. As she got near Wally she rubbed his shoulder and said, "I know, but you had my brother come home to help you help Mom, so get on with it." When she reached the door she added, "And when he's done whatever you brought him back to do, I want him out of here." She left without looking back.

"Is she okay?" I asked Wally. He was still staring at the closed door.

"I don't think any of us are okay, but no, she's not okay," answered Wally. "She's had these nightmares as long as I've known her, but they used to bother her once every six weeks or so. And now, it's more like five times a week."

"What does it mean?"

Wally swung his chair around to face me. "As near as I can tell from searching the Internet, when nightmares increase like that it either means an increase in stress or that something from the unconscious is trying to break through."

"Well, there's certainly stress around here," I said.

Wally waved for me to follow him. He led me down the hall to Maggie's room where Oberon was recuperating. This room was smaller and darker than Mom's room, but other than that they were mostly identical; the same bed, the same chair near the bed, the same bureau. There were pictures and art pieces, many by Carol, all over Mom's walls, but there was nothing on Maggie's walls. When I was younger I thought it was strange that Maggie didn't add any personal touches to her room, so one Halloween I colored a picture of a black cat and hung it above her bed.

That black cat was still there on her wall. I hadn't noticed it before when I had been in here watching Oberon, but I noticed it then. I wondered if she wondered if I knew she was a black panther back then.

"Before you left, you confirmed that Oberon and Vernalisa were fighting the same poison," said Wally, bringing me back from my thoughts.

"I did?" I asked. "I don't recall saying that."

"Yes. Remember? You told Carol their spit smelled the same. Knowing that could be the key to an antidote."

"Great."

"It is great. All we need is for one of them to recover, and we can cure the other one with the antibodies the cured one produced as they recovered." Wally pointed at Oberon's bed. "I know he was poisoned more recently, but he seems to be further along in recovery. It may be because of his size or it could be that he received a smaller dose than your mother did, but either way he's the better candidate to be an antidote."

"So we wait until he wakes up," I guessed.

"Normally that's exactly what we'd have to do, but we have a secret weapon on our side."

"What?" I asked, but I should have known he was talking about me.

"Smell this," he said, handing me a small glass bottle.

I lifted the bottled to inspect its contents first. It was a small brown bottle with what looked like the cotton ends of several Q-tips inside. I unscrewed the top and lifted the bottle to my nose. I recognized the smell immediately. "The drool," I said.

"It is," he said. "Now go walk around outside. If you can find a plant that matches, then maybe we can speed up Oberon's recovery."

"Which will speed up Mom's recovery," I finished.

"That's the plan," said Wally. "So go do your thing."

I certainly didn't feel like much of a weapon, and I was about to discover that I wasn't much of a secret either.

CHAPTER 25

"WELL DONE, PEE-WEE"

"WHERE DO YOU THINK YOU'RE GOING?" asked Aunt Maggie as I exited the kitchen. She was standing on the back porch, although she never just stands. She was waiting for me.

"I'm going plant hunting," I told her.

"Not by yourself, you're not," she stated emphatically.

The finality of her tone threw me for a moment. "It's daylight," I said, pleadingly.

She nodded, but she wasn't looking at me. She was looking at the small barn. I looked where she was looking. When Aiden came out, Maggie turned to me and said, "He's going with you."

Going with Aiden was fine with me, but I was a bit unnerved by Maggie's insistence that he did.

As Aiden got close to the porch he called me by what I had decided was my wolf name, "Jazz-barr."

"Are you my bodyguard?"

He looked at Maggie and smiled. "I'm your guide. I think I know where to find what you're looking for."

"Oh, good. The way she sounded I thought I needed a bodyguard."

Aunt Maggie rolled her eyes and pointed at me. "Just stay with him."

I really wanted to say something clever back to her, but after she had her say, she went back inside. I suppose she was confident that I'd do as she ordered.

Aiden led me through the upper back pasture where Kitty and the bulk of our alpacas were. I noticed that Kitty didn't bark ferociously at Aiden anymore, but she didn't nuzzle up to him either. They had come to an understanding that he was not the threat she had thought. I noticed that she made a point of escorting us through the pasture by walking right next to me and between Aiden and myself.

When we left through the back gate I had to be careful to keep Kitty from following us out. Once I was on the other side of the fence Kitty whimpered.

Aiden grinned at my awkward dance getting through the gate without Kitty. "She doesn't trust us," Aiden told me.

"By 'us,' do you mean wolves?"

"Of course," he said. "Wolves and dogs have always been suspicious of each other."

"My father wrote about that in his journal," I told him. "According to Cherokee legend it was dogs that roamed free in the mountains and it was wolves that stayed with people. They each thought the other were better off. Is that the truth?" I asked.

Aiden laughed and put his arm around me. "Jazz-barr, I am old, but I don't think I'm as old as you think."

We walked like that through the field beyond the upper pasture, the same field where Carol first encountered Aayma. Thinking about her made me shudder. With what I knew of Aayma from experience, I found it impossible to think of her as Mom's daughter, much less as our sister. The feel of Aiden's arm, still across my shoulder, was comforting.

The bright of the day faded as we took our first steps out of the pasture and into the wooded area.

"Where to?" I asked as he let go of me so that I could step between two trees.

"I do not know, Jazz-barr. Like all wolves, my sense of smell is very strong. I know I have smelled something akin to what Mr. Wally put in your bottle, but it was as we ran through here. I haven't been able to find it again." He looked down. "I am sorry."

"We'll find it," I said, more to encourage him than to confess a strong conviction. "You're sure you were in these woods?" I asked.

"Yes."

"But you don't remember where?"

"No."

"It's okay." I meant it this time because I was thinking how Mr. Gabriel would think. "Just tell me what you remember."

He studied me with his eyes.

"Were you running uphill or downhill?"

"Flat," he smiled.

"Good." I smiled, too. "You see, you remember more than you thought. It was flat," I repeated. "Was it near a creek?"

He frowned. "I do not think so."

"That's okay. How about darkness? Was it daytime when you ran across the flat?"

"Yes."

"How dark was it?"

Looking around he said, "It was much darker than this, but I remember suddenly being assaulted by bright light. Maybe the sun came out from behind a dark cloud."

"Was it a cloudy day?"

"No." As he answered his chest sank again. "I am sorry."

"Aiden, it's okay, really. I think I know right where you were."

He frowned.

"I think you ran through a clearing. And I think I know where it is." There was only one sizable clearing in these woods that I knew of, and that was to our right. It was where my family picnicked. There was a small spring-fed creek that we could only wade in if it was really hot. The clearing was large enough for our family and another to spread out, and it was surrounded by patches of flowers. If there was going to be a spot with a large variety of vegetation it would be that clearing.

I led the way, which meant going straight into the woods until we came to the creek and then turning right. After that, all we had to do was follow the creek until we came to the clearing.

"What are you doing here, Jasper?"

I stopped and scanned around, frantically trying to identify where the voice was coming from. I should have just looked at Aiden. He knew, and he immediately placed himself between me and the voice.

Although I couldn't see her, I knew whose voice it was.

Aayma stepped out from behind an oak tree on the far side of the creek. "Go home, dog," she sneered at Aiden.

From behind him I could see the tension mounting in Aiden's neck and shoulders.

"What do you want?" Aiden growled back at her.

"Oww," she patted her chest. "You're so scary," she mocked.

"I don't care if you're scared," he said. His breathing was louder and his whole body leaned toward her. "Just leave."

She walked leisurely to the edge of the creek across from us and put her hands on her hips. "Me . . . leave? Why would I want to miss all this fun?" Then in a deeper, more commanding voice she barked, "Jasper!"

I stepped to the side so that I was still behind Aiden, but not directly behind him. "Wad?"

She smirked. "When you talk like that, you reveal yourself, boy."

I just stared at her.

"You were told to leave and you did. Now you're back, but you can leave again. I want you gone, Jasper. Gone!"

I still just stared. I was too scared to speak. Actually, I was too scared to think.

"Go ahead and test me if you must," said Aayma. "But I wouldn't." With that she lifted her arm and twirled a small circle with her right finger.

Six hyenas emerged from the underbrush behind her. They walked slowly to the edge of the creek and stood on either side of her watching us.

It was a human Aiden and me squared off against Aayma and six hyenas. I was too scared to move. Aiden wasn't moving either. Across the creek the hyenas began to spread out. They were going to outflank us on either side, and they had the numbers to do it.

I thought it was hopeless until I heard the pack barking in the distance. They were coming. Aiden and I both looked in the direction where the barking was coming from. I think the hyenas looked, too. It was surely an unpleasant sound to them.

But Aayma didn't look. She didn't flinch either. When the rest of us were distracted by the pack en route, she seized that as the ideal moment to attack. "Go!" she ordered.

Aiden turned toward me and yelled, "Climb!"

Luckily there was an old cedar tree with low enough branches that I could climb just ahead. I could hear the hyenas splash through the creek as I sprinted for the cedar. I lunged for a branch that was maybe eight feet off the ground. With a grip over my head I was able to get my feet under me and onto some lower branches. Once I was established inside the tree, climbing was like climbing a ladder. Only when I scrambled up enough to be out of jumping range from the hyenas did I dare to look back.

Aiden had not followed me up the tree as I had expected. He was at the base of the cedar. His shirt was off, and he was in wolf form. He was much larger than the hyenas, but there were six of them and they were circled around him.

The barking told me that the pack was getting closer, but I couldn't see them yet. I could do nothing to help Aiden but anticipate the other wolves.

"Get on with it!" screamed Aayma.

The hyena farthest to our left charged straight at Aiden. Being larger and stronger Aiden easily absorbed the direct impact and flipped the smaller animal over on his back. Aiden had him by the neck and pinned him to the ground. The hyena yelped out in pain, which brought the other hyenas swarming all over Aiden. They knocked Aiden from atop his foe and bit at his underbelly as he rolled away. They were in a frenzied state as they lunged and snipped from different directions. All Aiden could do was snap at them to keep them a bit at bay, but he couldn't do any real damage that way. They'd have eventually worn him down if they had had time, but the pack was getting closer and louder.

It was no more than a fraction of a second between the moment when I saw the pack and when they overran the hyenas. They washed over those hyenas like a wave washing over a sandcastle on the beach. Those hyenas rolled and slid, they whimpered and cried, but mostly they scrambled to their feet and ran.

The wolves ran in pursuit—all the wolves except Maire, that is. She stayed and tended Aiden, who had gotten to his feet. He didn't move much, but what movements he made were tentative and strained.

I watched them from above. There was an unmistakable connection between them as he found his bearings and she encouraged him. It was soothing to watch them, and I found myself relaxing as I did. That relaxing feeling disappeared when I looked down and saw a black mamba snake slithering toward them. They couldn't see the snake, and I was afraid that if I yelled to them it would strike, so I had no choice but to do what I did. I threw myself down on that snake. As I dropped I pulled my legs up under me, and I tried to time it so that when I hit the ground with the force of my jump I'd be adding the force of a stomp as well. Luckily, I landed on it with both feet. Unluckily, my kick-as-I-landed strategy had the effect of forcing my ankles to absorb all the force of the impact.

"*Ow!*" I screamed as I collapsed.

I fell to the left of the snake, landing flat on my back. Before I could move, Maire nosed my feet off the snake. She picked it up just behind the head and shook it violently. The way it flopped in her mouth I knew it had no life in it.

The sound of clapping came from across the creek. It was Aayma. "Well done, pee-wee, well done. You've escaped again. Just how long do you think you can be this lucky?"

I wanted to tell her, "As long as it takes," but she wasn't there anymore.

CHAPTER 26

FOXGLOVE

AIDEN AND I LIMPED HOME with armloads of raspberry-colored flowers. The tiny bell-shaped flowers were all around the perimeter of the picnic clearing growing wild. I remember them from our picnic days because the bees loved them and would climb inside the bell. Once when I was six, I stuck my nose in the wrong one and got stung right between the eyes. My face got so puffy that the kids at school called me the Stay-Puff Marsh-mallow Man.

"You're sure?" asked Wally when we entered his makeshift lab in the birthing barn.

"We're sure," I said.

Aiden nodded his agreement.

Carol was there behind him. "That's foxglove," she said as we lay our bundles on a bench.

"It is," agreed Wally.

"I could have gone out for that," she declared with an exaggerated displeasure.

"You can go for more if we need more, but we needed Jasper to tell us if it was a match."

"Oh, my," I whined. "Was I supposed to get a match?"

Aiden frowned at me. He knew very well that after our ordeal

115

with the hyena I spent fifteen minutes sniffing flowers in search of a match.

"That was sarcasm," I explained.

"Very amusing," he muttered as he left.

Carol waited until the door closed behind Aiden and then asked Wally, "Are you done with him now?"

Wally had taken three of the flower stalks and was moving toward a lab table when he answered, "I hope so. We'll know by morning."

Carol pointed at me. "And then you're gone. Do you hear me?"

Wally wheeled his chair around to face us. "Why don't both of you go?"

"You don't need any help?" asked Carol in a softer tone than she had used with me.

"I'm fine."

"I'll bring you some dinner," she said. Stepping toward me she slid her hand through my arm and turned me toward the door. "Let's go check on Mom."

I flinched pivoting on my ankle as I turned to follow her out.

"Jasper, what did you do?" asked Carol, putting one hand on my stomach and the other on my back. She was going to hold me up if I needed it.

I started to tell her about my encounter with Aayma, but looking at her I thought better of it. "I wisted my angle in de boods," I told her.

She didn't let go of me, but she leaned back to look me in the eyes. "What's wrong?"

I hadn't realized that my words had gone haywire on me again until I looked at Wally and saw that he was looking at me like he had heard it, too. "Why?" I asked stalling.

I took a deep breath. Talking slowly and deliberately I said, "I'm just worried about Mom."

"Oh, really," said Carol with her right eyebrow up and that extremely irritating head bob she does when she knows I know she caught me. "You got worried about Mom now, but a minute ago you were joking around with sarcasm."

"We ran into Aayma in the woods," I confessed.

Carol let go of me and then punched me in the arm.

"I'm sorry," I told her, rubbing my arm.

"Sorry," she repeated. "Sorry for what?"

"Look, you two," said Wally. "I'm working here."

"This is your fault, too," she snapped at him.

"Yes, it is," he said. "And now I'd like to make sure that the danger we all risked is worth it."

Carol huffed. I could tell she had plenty more to say by the way she churned her jaw back and forth. "I'll be back with your dinner in a while," she said again, this time without warmth.

"She's mad," I said when she was gone.

"She's not mad," Wally corrected me as he slid his wheelchair up to his workbench. "She's scared."

CHAPTER 27

LOOKING LIKE HER

WHEN I GOT TO THE HOUSE there was no one in the kitchen. On the counter was a package of ground beef thawing. I pressed my finger on it and felt the squish beneath the plastic wrap. It was pretty well thawed, which meant dinner would be sooner rather than later. I looked around for other hints about the dinner menu, but found none. I did that more from habit than hunger.

Mom's room was next. She was sleeping soundly, but this time she was on her side facing the door. I got excited thinking she had rolled herself on her side because the last time I saw her she just lay on her back. Rushing over to the side of her bed I knelt down on my knees to be even with her face.

"Mom," I whispered very softly.

Her eyes didn't open.

Leaning my chest against the edge of her bed, I studied her face. Other than the little drool on her cheek she looked like she always looked. She looked different, too, but I think that's because I'd never looked at her from this distance before. I'd watched her closely a million times, but almost always that was to watch for her reaction to something. The reactions I was most on the lookout for were either to see if I disappointed her or pleased her.

From six inches I noticed her skin was fairer than I thought. I remembered she hadn't been in the sun for days and days. Maybe that was why. As I looked at her I wondered if she'd ever gone a full day without being in the sun. I nearly laughed at myself as I noted how much my mother loved the outdoors. Here's a newsflash: Mother Nature loves the outdoors.

I noticed something else from six inches away. My mother has freckles. They are small and faint and mostly just go from one cheekbone across her nose to the other cheekbone. Just to see how much difference it would make, I pushed myself as far from the bed as my back would bend. From there I could just barely see the freckles.

Leaning closer again I folded my arms on the edge of the bed and began talking to her the way I had always talked to her. I told her, "Wally's working on an antidote for you." And I told her, "Carol's mad at me." Then I added, "Wally thinks she's more scared than mad, but it still comes out to me as mad."

I didn't look at Mom's face as I told her my thoughts. I didn't want to see her not looking back. Instead I looked at a couple of strands of her hair on her shoulder. They moved ever so slightly as she breathed.

If she'd been awake I'd have told her how scared we all were. Of all the things I was afraid of, losing her was at the top of the list. That was the fear that none of us dared say out loud. It was the fear I ran from all day. It was the fear that haunted those last minutes before I went to sleep and sometimes kept me from sleeping at all.

My thoughts drifted to her hair. Maybe my thoughts drifted away from where they were, but either way I was thinking about her hair then. She had long, thick, wavy black hair that smelled like honeysuckle. Right then her hair was tied up on the back of her head. Someone, either Maggie or Carol, had tied her hair up to be out of the way.

Having her hair that way may have been convenient, but it wasn't Mom. Mom wore her hair down. I had to stand up to reach over her to untie her hair and make it right. I took my time fluffing it and arranging it. I left most of it spread out behind her. I put a handful over her shoulder and stepped back to admire my work.

"Now you look like you," I told her.

I leaned back over and put my face down next to her head. I took a long slow breath. That's when I lost it.

CHAPTER 28

CAROL ON THE ROOF

"WHY DID YOU UNDO HER HAIR?"

The question startled me. I didn't realize that Maggie was behind me. Wiping my eyes with my sleeve, I stood up quickly and turned around slowly. "I'm looking for Carol?"

She didn't give me one of those looks that said, "I know you know you didn't answer my question." She didn't look at me at all. What she did was step close to me and hold out her hand.

I dropped the stretchy thing from Mom's hair into the palm of her hand.

As soon as she had it she stepped around me and bent over Mom. "We have the Mother's hair up to cool the back of her neck. Your sister is on the roof."

I climbed the stairs to where Carol was on the roof. The top of our house was built so that there was a long, thin, flat strip where the peak of the roofline would have been. The angled part of the roof was built up around it, so when Mom stood up there, the roofline came up just above her waist. Mom called it an observation deck, but the rest of us just called it "the roof." In my family it was a right of passage to be allowed up there without a grown-up. That was the seventh grade for me.

Linus liked to go up there when a storm was coming. He took

me with him a couple of times when I was in grade school, but that ended when Carol told on him. Mom was real mad that he took me up there when it was windy. I blamed myself that he had gotten in trouble, but Linus never treated me differently. All he ever said about it was, "You just need more weight, and that's not a problem for someone who eats like you do."

I miss him.

Carol was sitting on the floor of the roof facing the door when I got there. Her head was down, but she lifted it when she heard me.

"What are you doing?" I asked.

"I'm dancing in the moonlight," she answered.

That was an odd answer for her. Sarcasm was not her style. She preferred direct and blunt.

I generally liked sarcasm, but I didn't like it when Carol did it. Now that I think about it, I don't really ever like sarcasm when it's aimed at me.

I stood next to the wall she was leaning her back against and looked out over the back pastures. From up there I could have seen that encounter between Aayma and Carol that freaked Carol out so much. As I thought of that, I looked over toward the woods where I had just encountered her. The woods were too thick for me to see the clearing where we got Wally's flowers, but I wondered if Aayma was still out there somewhere. When I looked back down at Carol she was staring up at me.

"We're all scared," I told her as I sat down next to her.

"I know everyone thinks I'm wrong," she said, looking straight ahead. "Even my husband thinks I'm letting my fear get the best of me."

This was one of those moments when I realized that there were some blessings in having my speech problems. I knew that I wanted to say something comforting and clever, but since I didn't know anything comforting or clever to say, I kept my mouth shut. It was the right move.

"We are no match for her, Jasper." Carol turned her head to face me. Looking deep and hard at me she said, "We just aren't. Look what she did to Mom."

Carol stared at me again. I thought she was going to wait until I said something, so I said, "Mom's going to be okay."

Carol rolled her eyes and looked away from me. "Of course she's going to be okay. But she needs time to be okay and as long as you stayed in Richmond, *she* was giving us time." That reference was to Aayma.

"You really don't trust her, do you?" I asked.

"I don't have a choice, Jasper. We have to do whatever it takes to get Mom back."

"What if it takes getting an antidote?"

She shrugged. "I hope that's what it takes, since that's the strategy *we've all* decided on." When she said the words, "we've all," her voice got whiny and nasal. It was more sarcasm. "That's why I left."

I didn't understand. "That's why you left?" I repeated.

"That's why I left Wally to work by himself. If we're going to defy Aayma and work on that antidote, then we need to do it quickly, so I need to get out of the way." She looked back at me, her eyes narrowing to slits. "And you need to go back to Richmond."

I stared back at her.

"Tonight," she said.

"I don't think that's a good idea," I told her.

A tear rolled down her cheek.

"What's wrong," I asked.

More tears rolled down her cheeks. She swallowed hard and shook her head back and forth slowly. "I'm just trying to honor

Mom, but I'm not up to it." She wiped her eyes with her finger-tips. "The last thing Mom said to me before she slipped away was that it's my time." Frowning, Carol repeated, "'It's my time.' What does that mean anyway? With Dad gone and Linus gone I assumed that Mom meant I was to take charge in her absence. Maggie says that's what Mom meant, too, but I'm not sure I want to be the matriarch of this family." She exhaled loudly. "And no one else does either."

I stayed quiet.

Rubbing her hands nervously, Carol said, "I don't want Wally to think I don't have confidence in him finding an antidote, because I'm sure he can." She exhaled loudly again. "I'm just afraid it will take too long."

Until that moment I hadn't thought about anything other than if it would work or not. I just knew it would. I knew what Wally could do, and if he said he could work up an antidote with fox-glove, then he could. But he was also slow. He would call it methodical, but it was slow. And methodical or not, slow was a problem. Aayma was not above attacking us. She had been behind Riley's kidnapping. If we counted that kidnapping, then she'd made four runs at me, two today.

On the other hand, we had Aiden and the pack.

"If Aayma decides to overrun us, Jasper, then we won't be able to stop her." Carol pointed at me and added, "That was her threat, and she meant it."

"If that's the problem, then we need to get ready for her." I couldn't really believe that I had said that. I sounded more like Aiden, or even Linus. It sure didn't sound like me.

It didn't sound like me to Carol either. She just frowned and shook her head. "If Linus were here it would be his time, and gearing up for war would be his call. But he's not here, Jasper. I'm here, and gearing up for war is not my call. I want us to buy time until Mom is back. That's why you have to leave. That's why you have to leave soon." She looked at her watch, "It's nearly five o'clock. I want you driving out of here before it gets dark so that Aayma can still see you leave."

"I can't do that, Carol."

"You can, and you will." Her speech was missing the whiny, apologetic quality that had been there and was replaced by a strong, crisp tone.

I held up my hands, palms out, and said, "I haven't told you yet what happened on the road this morning."

"Go on," she said.

"Do you remember telling me to wait until daylight?"

She nodded yes.

"Well, I might not have done that."

Her lips pressed together.

"Do you remember the dream you had this morning?" I continued.

"The dream where some vultures attacked you on the side of the road?" she said, her eyes still narrow.

"I'm not sure it was a dream."

"If it wasn't a dream, what was it?" She didn't wait for an answer. "I saw you throw something."

"My sandwich."

"I saw you fall back and one of the vultures jumped on your back."

I nodded, waiting for her to go on, but she went back to having her eyes dart all over.

"Do you know what happened next?"

Shaking her head no, she said, "I saw everything from way high up and then I fell. That's when I woke up. It had to be a dream." She looked at me, pleading with her eyes. "How could it be anything other than a dream? I was here. I was here in my bed, and you were in Richmond." She stared off again. "It felt so real."

"It was real. I can't explain it, but everything you saw happened. And you saw it happen. I was hoping you could tell me what happened next."

"Jasper, this is crazy. How can I tell you what happened? I wasn't there."

"But I think, maybe, you were there."

She shook her head slowly. "Do you know how nuts that sounds?"

"This?" I asked. "You think *this* is what sounds nuts? Our barn is full of humans who are actually Russian wolves with Irish names." I pointed over my shoulder with my thumb. "There's a family of wolverines in Richmond watching out for Riley, and, oh yeah, our Mom is Mother Nature." I leaned back against the wall feeling clever. "But this, this is what sounds nuts."

Carol half smiled. "And you didn't mention having a black panther for a nanny."

It was pleasant to make light of all that for a moment. It was nice to see Carol relax enough to join in. But it didn't last long before we returned to serious business.

"So driving at night isn't safe," observed Carol.

"No," I said. "What about your dreams?"

"Why do you want to know?"

"Something saved me, Carol. And I think it was you. That vulture was on top of me, and something hit it. I felt it. It felt like a big hand snatched it off my back. I felt the impact, and then it was gone. You saw everything else. Why didn't you see that?"

"I don't know, and I don't want to talk about it."

"Doesn't that strike you as odd?"

"What?"

"That you're afraid to just talk about it?"

"I'm not afraid, Jasper," she replied, just before all the color drained out of her

head. Her face froze as she stared at something over my shoulder.

"Holy mackerel!" I blurted as I turned to see what she was looking at. A gigantic eagle had landed and was perched on the edge of the roof just over my left shoulder. It stared down at me as I scrambled away. It didn't have discernable eyebrows, but as it watched me use my feet to slide my butt across the floor, it clinched its eyebrows and tipped its head to the side.

When I was far enough away that it couldn't reach out and grab me, I looked back at Carol. She was still frozen and staring.

"Carol," I whispered. She didn't respond. "Carol," I said a little louder. Again I got no response, so I reached out and touched her right arm just below the elbow. She jumped enough to lift herself off the floor. Her head snapped in my direction.

The eagle dropped down to the floor near my feet.

That was it for Carol. She pushed herself up off my left shoulder and sprinted for the door.

I watched her disappear and then I looked back at the eagle. It had watched her as long as I had, and when she was gone the eagle took flight without a glance at me.

CHAPTER 29

DOMINIONS

AUNT MAGGIE AND I HAD THE KITCHEN to ourselves through dinner. Carol fixed two big bowls of shepherd's pie and took them to Wally's lab. Neither of us said anything about what had happened on the roof.

When Maggie made shepherd's pie, which wasn't often enough for me, it was meat and vegetables in brown gravy covered with mashed potatoes and baked. What made it different each time was the vegetables she put in with the meat. Maggie said her recipe called for whatever vegetables she had either too much of or not enough. Once she put Brussel sprouts in with the meat. Even Mother Nature won't eat Brussel sprouts. Tonight the vegetables were peas, carrots, and onions: no leftovers.

Maggie wasn't what you'd call a talker, so eating in silence was what we did. When I got myself a second serving Maggie stayed and sat with me.

"Can I ask a question?" I asked.

"Of course."

"Why did you tell me to wait until daylight to travel?"

Maggie looked at me hard. If I didn't know her better I would have said she was angry, but I knew she was just getting serious. "Tell me again what happened."

"Okay," I said, but I didn't see the point. "I woke up early, and it was still dark when I left."

"What came after you?" she asked.

"It was a couple of vultures."

She nodded.

"The wolverines were there?" she asked.

"What makes you think it was the wolverines? Maybe I got away all by myself."

"Did you?" she asked immediately.

"No, but it wasn't the wolverines that protected me." I hesitated, trying to think through what to say next.

"I sent the wolverines," said Maggie. "So if it wasn't them, what was it?"

"I don't know, but something came out of the sky and snatched one off my back. I was face down so I didn't see it, but I think Carol did."

I waited for Maggie to react to what I just said, but she didn't.

"Carol saw most of it in a dream, but she says she didn't see that." Again I waited for a reaction from Maggie, but she just watched me.

Finally I just asked, "Can you explain any of this to me?"

"What?"

"What's the deal with the daylight? And what's up with Carol? Did she fly to Richmond?"

"No. Carol cannot fly."

"Well, how'd she see what happened to me in Richmond?"

Maggie's eyes narrowed while we stared at each other. Eventually she said, "Carol has to make peace with who she is, as do you."

"Me?" I jumped. "What do I have to do?"

She smiled at me. It was a pity smile. "To whom more is given, more is expected."

"'To whom more is given, more is expected,'" I repeated. "Okay." I thought I might explode. I was desperately asking Maggie questions, and she was answering me in riddles.

"It is more difficult for humans. You are all so different."

That seemed funny to me. Maggie was the most different human I knew.

"For wolves, they are children for two years and then they must find their place in the pack. Their place in the pack determines what they do. Their pack has dominion over a territory, and by simply being in the pack and doing what they do, they serve the Mother and the Father."

"'The Father'?" I frowned. "My father?"

"No. The Father. The Creator."

"'The Creator,'" I repeated. My mother had spoken of a creator all my life, but I had never thought of him as Father. I suppose I had always thought of him as him, but I didn't know why. And I certainly didn't know why the word "Father" would apply. Father was closer, more personal, than Creator. If he was Father, where was he? I asked Maggie, "Why have I never seen him then?"

"Do you know what to look for?"

I naturally thought I was looking for someone who looked like my father, but as soon as Maggie asked that, I wondered. "I guess not," I admitted. "Do you?"

"Not in the way you mean, but I know that he is by what I see."

I nodded like I understood, but I didn't.

"Wolves do not *see* winter coming, but they see *that* it is coming. They may not know what they are looking for, but they know it when they see it. It is the same with the Creator."

I felt we had strayed too far from my questions and too far over my head. "What about Carol and me?"

"For the wolf, he needs to know what his place in the pack is and what the packs' dominion is. For you and Carol, you need to know what your dominion is, too. Do you know your dominion?"

"I don't even know what a dominion is, Maggie. How could I know what mine is?"

"You know what the Mother's dominion is, do you not?" she asked.

"Nature," I said, trying to imagine the answer she was looking for, as I was still rather lost. I knew my mother had power or powers that we had no idea about. I knew that animals obeyed her, some to the point of becoming human when she wanted. But did the earth obey her like that? Did the weather? I had no idea.

"Nature," she said strongly. "Now, Jasper, what about you?"

"Me? What about me?"

"What is your dominion?"

"I don't have a dominion. Nothing serves me like you serve Mom." When I realized what I had said, another question came to my mind. "If my mother's domain is all of nature, how come vultures and black mambas go against her?"

"That is simple, Jasper," she said. "Animals—all animals—behave according to their nature. They obey their nature, if you want to put it that way, and they have no choice to do otherwise. When they do otherwise, it is always because they are diseased. This is how men put it, and it is correct."

"Rabies," I said to myself out loud.

"Yes, rabies. But humans are different. Humans can choose to behave in ways other than their nature. That is what we are speaking about. You and Carol are by nature humans, but humans—each human—has a dominion."

"I do not see how that could be. How could all humans be in charge?"

Maggie closed her eyes and took a long, slow breath. "You are thinking about your dominion as your kingdom, with you as the king and everyone else as your subjects."

I didn't say, "Of course," but that's exactly what I thought.

"Your dominion is your responsibility. Humans do not rule over creation, but they are responsible for creation. Humans are responsible in a way that no animal is or could be. Your dominion is a unique part of creation that you, Jasper, are responsible for."

I remembered what Mr. Gabriel had said about being true to the real you. "Am I supposed to know the answer to that now? I'm just a kid."

She stood up and patted me on the cheek. "Some young wolf pups must be ready for winter sooner than other wolf pups, but winter comes when it comes."

"Maggie," I said, looking up at her. "You're a black panther, aren't you?"

"Indeed."

"Then why are all your examples about wolves instead of about panthers?"

She tipped her head back and snorted, which was the way she laughed. "That was for you, Jasper. For you."

CHAPTER 30

THE FIRST ANTIDOTE

NO SOONER HAD MAGGIE LEFT the room than Wally entered. In his lap was a small box. Carol came in right behind him carrying two dinner plates, one untouched and the other hardly touched.

"He did it," announced Carol.

"Really?" I asked. I realized that I had reacted without thinking that Wally might think I doubted him, but I wished I could have taken it back when I noticed Carol flinch.

"We'll know soon enough," Wally said. If my question had bothered him, he didn't show it.

A new, disturbing thought occurred to me. "What are you going to do next?" I asked.

"I've got enough of this," he said, patting the box on his lap, "to give both Vernalisa and Oberon a dose. I'll have more ready later tonight."

"But you're hoping Oberon will get better sooner, and then you'll use his blood to make an even better antidote, right?"

"That's the plan," he said. "Your mother has been fighting this longer, but we don't know how much venom either of them is fighting, and we don't know if Mother Nature's system is a bit different from other humans either. So it really could be either of them that responds best to the foxglove."

"You realize that Mom's biology might be a little different from other humans', but what about Oberon?"

"Well," said Wally with a serious look on his face, "I've adjusted the dosages based on their weight. He's quite a bit bigger than your average human."

"What's the matter, Jasper?" asked Carol.

"I don't think Oberon is human," I answered.

"I thought we already had this conversation," said Carol.

"We did, but we didn't know what he was," I said. "But I think I know now."

Wally and Carol looked at me, waiting for me to go on.

"When I was in Richmond I saw some bears. They smelled like Oberon. I texted Wally, but that was when he called me to come home, so I think the message got lost."

"Okay, he's a bear," said Carol. "Maggie's a black panther."

"And we've got a bunkhouse full of wolves," added Wally.

"And we know who they serve," I said. Pointing at Wally's box I said, "If you give that to Oberon and he wakes up, we could have a bear on our hands and we don't know if he's Mom's servant or Aayma's."

Carol's eyes got bigger. "We can't risk it," she said.

Wally and Carol stared at each other for a long moment. I think Wally was considering what to do. Finally he said, "It is a risk, I admit it, but I think it's a risk we need to take. First of all, I think it's unlikely that he's on the other side because they attacked him."

"That could have been a mistake," countered Carol, "or they could have done that to deceive us."

"True," said Wally, "but unlikely, I think. The other reason I think it's worth the risk is that it might be our best shot at bringing your mother out of it." He looked at me, "Besides, we can restrain him now, while he's still comatose."

I looked at Carol. The worry on her face told me how she'd vote. "I say we go for it."

Wally looked at Carol, but she wasn't looking at either of us anymore. She was putting their plates on the counter. Her back was toward us as she got plastic wrap out. In a chilly voice she said, "Do what you have to do."

CHAPTER 31

"NO!"

SURPRISINGLY, MAGGIE AGREED WITH CAROL. She agreed, that is, when it was too late to matter. She had watched Wally give Vernalisa her shot, and then she watched Oberon get his. It wasn't until after that that she heard about the restraints and why we were using them.

"A bear," she had said. "The Mother has never called on a bear before. Bears are loners. Their loyalty is unpredictable."

Luckily for us all, these comments were not made in front of Carol, who, at the time, was in Mom's room.

"Does Aayma call on bears?" I asked.

"I don't think so," answered Maggie. "Scavengers are more to Aayma's liking."

"Well," said Wally, "since we've already done it, and since we're prepared for it being bad, let's go ahead and act like it will be good."

Maggie nodded. "I agree. I will say nothing to alarm Miss Carol, but I will watch the bear through the night. It will not do to have him loose and inside if he is wrong."

"And if he is wrong?" asked Wally.

"I will do what I need to do," said Maggie in a way that put a chill up my spine.

"How was your trip home?" asked Riley on the phone. I was glad she called. I had texted her and told her to call if she could when I went upstairs, but that was thirty minutes earlier, so I thought she might have gone to bed already.

"It was fine," I lied. "I got home about lunchtime."

"Have you seen Harlan and the rest of them?"

"No. They put me to work as soon as I got home. Maggie had a list for me. How was your day?"

"My dad talked to your brother-in-law tonight," she said in an apologetic voice that made me assume it wasn't such a good thing.

"Yeah," I said.

"Dad wasn't going to tell me about it, but I overheard some of the conversation. He didn't want me to get my hopes up, but your brother-in-law told him the police might catch whoever has been threatening us. If they do, I might be coming back to Boone."

"*Really*?" I bolted up off the bed in excitement. I completely put it out of my mind that everything that Wally told her dad was complete bull. I figured what he meant was that the threat would be resolved as soon as Mother Nature was Mother Naturing again.

"'Maybe' is what he said," said Riley. "He said you were helping with an antidote for some kind of snakebite."

"That's true," I told her.

"My dad thinks you three make a good team, and I know if it weren't for me, he'd be right there with you." By "three," he meant Wally, her dad, and me.

"What do you mean, 'If it weren't for you'?"

"Come on, you know what I mean. The only reason we're in

Richmond is because of that threat. He's worried about something else happening to me."

"'Come on,' yourself, Riley. That threat wasn't about you. It was about making pharmaceuticals."

"I'm the reason he let the threat run him out of Boone. If it weren't for me, he would still be there."

She was probably right, so I didn't bother arguing with her anymore. "But when the threat's gone, you'll be coming back, right?"

"When and *if,*" she said.

We talked another ten minutes, but I don't remember what we said. What I remember is what she said as we hung up. "I love you. Don't forget me."

Like I could.

It was a pretty full day. I had a half a day's drive, I got attacked by Aayma's minions twice, I watched Carol freak out two or three times, and I learned that what might be another threat could wake up downstairs anytime. Who could drift off to sleep with all that going through your mind? But I went to sleep smiling as I thought about what Riley had said.

When I came downstairs for breakfast the next morning, there was none, but the back door to the kitchen was wide open. I could hear voices coming from down the hall toward the room where Oberon was. Before I got there Maggie marched out, followed closely by Carol with Wally close behind her.

Aunt Maggie passed by me with a quick, "Good morning." She had her usual all-business demeanor going.

"He's a bit better," Carol said as she took me by the elbow and turned me around. "We just gave him a second dose of your foxglove antidote, and we're on our way to give Mom hers."

"He's better," I said. "That's great. That means it's working, right? Is he constrained, you know, just in case?"

"He is. Maggie saw to that," answered Carol. "I'll let Wally answer the 'Is it working' question."

"We're of a mixed mind about that, I'm afraid," said Wally. "He is better, but only a little, and according to Maggie he would have improved that much without the injection."

"That's still good though, right?" I asked, hoping that the sooner Oberon kicked it, the sooner Wally could use him to make an antidote for Mom.

"Of course it is. It's just that we don't know if the foxglove is having an effect."

"*NO!*" Maggie screamed.

We all flinched and turned toward the scream. I think my heart stopped. Assuming Maggie was in Mom's room, we all bolted in that direction, but as we crossed the kitchen we could see that Maggie was there.

Aiden and Maire were in the kitchen, too. Aiden was standing in the middle of the room holding a limp Kitty in his arms.

I don't know about Carol or Wally, but for me my first reaction was relief that it wasn't Mom Maggie had yelled about. My second reaction, which came like a second domino falling after the first was tipped, was guilt for not being more concerned about Kitty, which was where my emotional merry-go-round ended up.

While I was circling through my emotions Maggie ran out the back door. Carol rushed over to cradle Kitty's head in her arms.

"She's breathing," yelled Carol for Wally and me. Then she pointed at the kitchen table.

Aiden gently placed Kitty on the table.

"Do you know what happened?" asked Wally.

"We found her in the far pasture this morning," said Maire. "She was lying down next to one of the alpacas."

"She was barely breathing," added Aiden. "That is why we brought her here." He looked at Wally. "We hoped your medicine would heal her."

Carol was busily combing through Kitty's coat looking for bite marks. When Aiden said what he said, she looked up and asked, "And the alpaca?"

Maire shook her head slowly.

"Was it Cranberry or Mrs. Jones?" asked Carol. Cranberry and Mrs. Jones were the two alpacas that Carol got to name because she had been on duty when they were born, a task that overwhelmingly fell to Maggie.

"We don't know," answered Aiden. "Maggie went to check on her kids."

Maggie sometimes referred to the alpacas as her kids.

"I assume it was a bite," said Wally to Carol. "If you can find the bite marks we might be able to tell if it was another black mamba bite. It'll help if we know what we're dealing with."

"We know," said Maire, lifting her arm. She had been holding something in her hand all along, but with everything else going on we hadn't noticed. It was hard not to notice it now as Maire held the dead snake up and let it dangle limply from her grip. I'd say it was around five feet long.

"This was under the dog when we got there," explained Maire.

"This is great," said an excited Wally.

The statement earned him an immediate scowl from everyone in the room.

Holding up his palms he said, "I know, that sounded bad. I don't mean that it's great that we lost one of the kids or that it's great that Kitty's hurt."

"Well, what *did* you mean, Wally?" asked Carol, a bit irritated.

"If there was just one snake and it bit Kitty second, then Kitty may have gotten a very small dose of the venom. If that's true, then her body might fight it off pretty quickly." He spread his hands. "If Kitty comes out of it before Oberon, we might be able to make an antidote from her."

Carol didn't acknowledge what Wally said before she took charge. Pointing at me, she said, "Drag Kitty's bed down to Mom's room." To Aiden she said, "Give Jasper a minute and take her down to my mother's room. Do you know where her room is?"

Aiden nodded yes.

"Wally," continued Carol, "how long will it take you to get a dose of your foxglove antidote ready for Kitty?"

"It's ready now. I just need to load it into a hypodermic needle." He started rolling out the door, but stopped to ask, "What do you think Kitty weighs, about 100 pounds?"

"There's a scale in Mom's bathroom," I offered.

Looking back at me Carol said, "Pull it out to the middle of the floor for Aiden after you get Kitty's bed down there." She clapped her hands twice. "Let's get moving, guys."

Kitty weighed 102 pounds and got her shot just after Mom got hers.

CHAPTER 32

"WE NEED YOUR DOMINION"

CAROL, WALLY, AND I WERE STILL IN MOM'S ROOM when Maggie returned. Maire came to get us.

"The panther is back," said Maire solemnly. "She wants everyone in the kitchen."

Maggie's sweater was on inside out. She must have been in a hurry when she got back from checking on her kids, which she must have done as the panther. Once we were all assembled, Maggie said, "I have combed the pastures. Last night they killed three of my babies: Bagel, Olive, and Mischief. Starburst and Sneezy are both missing."

"Why would she do that?" asked Carol.

"It is a declaration of war," said Aiden. Maire nodded her agreement.

Maggie stared at Carol.

"Haven't we been at war already?" asked Carol, her voice sounding desperate.

"No," answered Aiden.

"We've been attacked," countered Carol.

"The attacks we've received in the past have been messages. If this was a message, one death would have been enough," observed Aiden.

142

"So this is different," said Wally.

"Yes," agreed Maggie.

"Tell us what to do," Carol said to Maggie.

Maggie looked at Aiden and then back at Carol. If some communication passed between Aunt Maggie and Aiden, it was pretty subtle.

"Decide," answered Maggie.

"Decide what?"

"War has been declared, Carol. There is only one decision to be made," said Aiden.

"There's always more than one decision to be made," said Carol.

"We are lost," said Aiden, shaking his head.

"The human has not said what her decision is. Give her time," said Maire.

"Why is it my decision? Somebody tell me that," demanded Carol.

Aiden and Maire looked immediately at Maggie. Maggie stared back at Aiden for a moment before turning to Carol. "You're the Mother's daughter. When the Mother is gone, you will be the Mother."

Carol sat down when she heard that. She didn't faint, nor did her legs buckle beneath her. She just sat down on the floor right where she was.

"Carol?" asked Wally, gently rolling up next to her.

Carol didn't answer him right away.

"Are you okay?" Wally tried again.

Carol looked at him and then at Aunt Maggie. "Am I okay?"

"You have to be," answered Aiden.

Maggie scowled at him and then sat down on the floor directly in front of Carol. "The Mother has protected you from all this." She looked up at me and added, "She has protected both

143

of you from all this." Glancing back at Carol she continued, "We did not see that Aayma was gathering forces. But she was. She was increasing her domain. At first we thought she just wanted to keep Jasper from using his gift to make cures, but now it is clear she wants more than that."

"What does she want?" asked Carol in a whiny voice.

"She wants the Mother's domain," answered Maggie.

"If she thinks she can take it, she will take it," added Aiden.

We all stared at Aiden, trying to find another meaning in his words other than what we all knew they meant.

Aiden squatted behind Maggie and said, "War is coming. We must be ready."

Carol scanned all our faces. She didn't stay long on my face, but I could see she was looking for something she wasn't finding. Pity wasn't exactly what I felt, but I was glad to be a son instead of a daughter.

Wally put his hand on Carol's shoulder, which seemed to relax her enough for her shoulders to unclench. She put her hand on top of Wally's and then said to Maggie, "Okay. Tell me what to do."

"You must tell us what to do," Aiden told her.

Carol looked at Maggie, who nodded her head to confirm what Aiden had said.

Maggie said, "We do not need to be told to behave according to our nature, but we can only go beyond our nature if we are obeying the human whose domain it is. Do you understand?"

"No," answered Wally for Carol. "We do not understand, but is this the time for explanation or action?"

Aiden stood up and smiled at Wally. "I think you understand. It is the time for action."

"What are we preparing for?" asked Wally.

Aiden answered. "Aayma knows we got the foxglove yesterday. She tried hard to stop us, but she couldn't. And she knows that you are healing the Mother with it."

"She'll want to stop that," said Wally.

"Yes," agreed Aiden.

"So it will be soon," sighed Wally.

"Tonight," said Aiden.

"But she was no match for the pack yesterday," I said.

Aiden smiled at me. "She will be stronger tonight."

"You see," explained Aunt Maggie, "it is only in the night that she can assert her will unnaturally over her servants. I'm sure she is gathering more of her disease-spreading vermin even now, and she will bend them to her will when night falls. Without the Mother we cannot increase our number as Aayma can hers."

"She said she'd overrun us," remembered Carol. "That's what she's going to do."

"We just need to hold her off long enough for the Mother to return," said Maire.

With that, Carol looked at Wally and kept looking at him when she said to all of us, "She'll return."

"Can we send the rest of the alpacas away?" asked Maggie. "We can get Lee Rankin to take some over at Apple Hill Farm in Banner Elk, and maybe the McLeishes from Dreamland in Meadowview, Virginia, to come get them. They'll both take good care of our babies. I just hope they have room."

"Do you need my permission?" asked Carol.

"Yes," said Maggie. "And we need you to ask them if they'll come get our babies."

"Me? Why?"

"Because they can't say no if you ask," explained Maire.

"Okay," said Carol, hanging onto the "y" in disbelief.

"What is your dominion?" Maire asked Carol.

I watched Carol closely as she contorted her face to make

sense of the question. It made more sense to me since Maggie and I had just talked about mine. I was pretty sure Carol had no idea what she was being asked.

"It would help if we knew from where help was coming," continued Maire.

"Do you have a dominion?" Carol asked me.

"I guess," I answered. "But I don't know what it is."

"You don't?" snapped Maire with a frown.

"No," I answered slowly, looking at her and Aiden. They were looking at me as if I should know something.

I pointed gingerly at them.

Aiden nodded his head yes.

Maire rolled her eyes and said, "If you send the pack out today we might be able to find another pack or some lone wolves that you could subjugate."

My head was still swimming with the knowledge that I had dominion over wolves when Maire told Carol, "We need your dominion."

CHAPTER 33

THE TOUCH

FOR THE REST OF THE DAY MAGGIE AND I corralled what was left of our alpacas. We were able to send fifteen to Dreamland in Meadowview. The rest went to Apple Hill Farm in Banner Elk. By four o'clock, they were all gone.

Carol and Wally spent the day inside tending to the growing number of patients. At four o'clock, as Maggie and I watched the last load of alpacas drive away, Carol came out the kitchen door with Mom's phone to her ear. When she put the phone in the back pocket of her jeans she waved us over to her.

"That was your friend, Rose, on the phone. She says her family will be here tomorrow," said Carol.

"Not today," I said, without attempting to disguise my disappointment.

"We're probably okay for tonight, don't you think?" Carol asked, almost pleading with Maggie.

"How's the Mother?" asked Maggie, ignoring Carol's question.

"No change, but both Oberon and Kitty are starting to get restless. Wally says that's a good sign."

"It is a good sign," agreed Wally, who had just come out the back door. "I'm going to give them another dose now and then a third at midnight." To Carol he said, "I could use a little help."

While they headed off to the lab, Aunt Maggie started working on dinner, and I sat with Mom. She looked the same, but I didn't think she was as feverish as she had been.

The evening was uneventful, but it was hardly calm. Not much conversation, and I can't remember what we ate. That's very unusual for me.

Around seven o'clock the wolves began to show some life. Aiden was the last to emerge from their barn/bunkhouse. "How is the Mother?"

"Stable," answered Carol.

"I think her fever's breaking," I said. My comment drew some scrutiny from Carol, but Maggie's response was to go see for herself.

Aiden cleared his throat, which was a signal for all the wolves to gather around him. They were all in their human forms. Once they were gathered around he said, "It looks like we are alone for tonight."

A smattering of snorts, huffs, and chortles passed through the pack.

I don't know who said what, but I heard several comments like, "Of course we're alone," and "Let them come."

Aiden waited until the rumbling stopped and then he said, "I want two patrols out at all time. Go in groups of three and stay just inside the perimeter. No pursuit."

"No pursuit?" countered one of the wolves.

The pack went silent as Aiden walked over to the wolf that had spoken. "Do you have any more questions, Barrett?" It was clear from Aiden's tone what the answer to the question was.

"No, sir," said the wolf, looking down.

"He is young," Maire explained to me in a whisper. "Had anyone else in the pack questioned Aiden right then, the response would have been much harsher."

"Even if it was you?" I asked her.

The question seemed to puzzle her. She tipped her head and frowned before saying, "I am his mate. It is expected that I have privileges the others do not have. It is also expected that I support him like no other." She turned her attention back to Aiden. "In the pack the alpha would only be challenged by the young, who do not know better yet, or one wishing to replace him."

"No pursuit," repeated Aiden. "We are defending the Mother tonight."

"The Mother," cheered several wolves, as three of the wolves stripped down to their skin. Once they were naked, they transformed into wolves. I watched it happened. I had been there when it happened before, but I'd never actually seen it happen. I expected to see a painful process, like I had seen in several movies, but I didn't see it at all. There was just one moment when they were naked men and the next moment when they were wolves.

"Go," ordered Aiden.

Each one, as they left, brushed up against me. I thought it was an accident the first time. I realized it wasn't an accident the second, and I was ready when the third one went by. I put my hand on the top of his head and let it ride down his back as he passed by. I watched as the three wolves trotted off and disappeared into the trees to the west of our compound.

When I looked around, I caught Aiden and Maire both watching me. "You learn fast," said Maire.

"What did I do?" I wondered. As near as I could tell I hadn't learned anything.

"You sent them off with . . ." Aiden struggled with what word to say. He looked at Maire for help.

"Confidence . . . strength . . . courage . . . purpose," said Maire, offering him several possibilities.

"Yes," said Aiden with a smile. "That's it."

"All I did was touch them," I said.

Aiden laughed. "Do you think you could have done more?"

Of course I thought I could do more, but I couldn't think of what more to do, so I didn't answer.

"Let me help you, Jazz-barr," offered Maire. "At that moment you could do nothing more."

"All I did was pet them as they went by." Once I said the word "pet" I had second thoughts about it. These wolves were not my pets, so I said, "I just touched them."

"Yes," said Aiden.

"Why does a touch from a human matter so much?" I asked.

Three more wolves were disrobing. When I asked my question they stopped in mid-action. One of them was squatting with his pants halfway down. The other wolves stared at me.

"A touch from a human is not what you bring, Jazz-barr," Aiden told me. "It is your touch that matters. Yours and the Mother's, that is. We do not belong to you, but we are yours. There's not a wolf in this pack that would not lay his life down for you."

"Or hers," added Maire.

I could feel my whole body change. My eyes felt bigger. That was partly because I felt like crying, but it was something else, too. I slowly looked from one face to the next around the pack, and every set of eyes held mine. Each face I came to nodded or bowed to confirm Aiden's claim. Part of me wanted to say, "No, not me, I'm a kid," but I knew better than to do that. With the exception of Maire, the only female, every one of these wolves looked like a grown man to me. Even Barrett, who Maire referred to as a pup, looked like a grown man.

"Go," said Aiden, ordering the next group of three wolves to begin their patrol of the perimeter. This time I was ready for them to brush by me. This time I stroked the first two like I had stroked the third one from the first group. The last one to go by me stopped and nuzzled the side of his head along my thigh. He was strong and he pushed against me hard enough to make me struggle to keep from stepping away.

I watched this group head off into the darkness of the trees. Before they were out of sight, I felt Aiden's hand on my shoulder. "You see, your touch may not matter to vultures or groundhogs, but it does matter to us."

"You may never understand why it matters," said Maggie. She had come back out through the kitchen door and was standing on the steps. "You just need to understand it does. It is your responsibility to use that knowledge wisely."

CHAPTER 34

FLEE OR DIE

IT WAS A LONG DAY, BUT IT WAS OVER, and I for one was ready for what Linus used to call the sleep of the dead. That was Linus. He was the soundest sleeper I ever saw. When Linus would go to sleep on the couch, Carol would entertain me by tickling his nose with a feather. He'd squirm and thrash and wiggle around, but he wouldn't wake up. I used to wonder if I could ever be that tired. Now I know.

It was only 9:30, but I was ready to go to bed. I closed out of *Call of Duty,* which I was losing anyway, and headed to the kitchen to say goodnight.

Carol and Aunt Maggie were sitting at the kitchen table when I turned the corner. It must have been a pleasant conversation because they both were smiling when I walked in.

"Hungry again?" asked Maggie.

"Always," Carol answered for me.

I hesitated to think of something clever, but I didn't have time because at that precise moment a riot broke out behind the house. We heard snarling and barking, which was unusual for the wolf pack. Barking is a defensive maneuver for a wolf. Attacks are strategically silent. The barking wasn't just the wolves, either.

There was another kind of bark, a more high-pitched and annoying bark.

Maggie was the first one out the back door. Carol and I were close behind her.

"Hyenas," said Maggie. Her voice was more nasal, and the word sort of rolled in disgust as she said it. She was looking toward the western end of the pasture. It was pretty dark, so I couldn't see them. I knew they were there, though, because I could see the pack racing in that direction.

"They came looking for my babies," continued Maggie.

"Well, we fixed that," said Carol.

Other than making a few phone calls I didn't remember Carol helping us with the alpacas all day, but I decided to keep that observation to myself.

"What's up?" asked Wally from inside the kitchen.

Carol opened the door, and Wally rolled out to join us. On his lap was the wooden box where he carried the syringes.

"Some of Aayma's minions came scrounging around looking for my babies," said Maggie. Pointing to the northwest she added, "The pack is taking care of them now."

"It's a good thing we got them all moved," observed Wally.

"It is," agreed Maggie as she went back inside.

"How'd it go?" asked Carol.

Wally first looked up at her and then down at the box on his lap. "Oh, fine. Still not much change for your mother and Kitty, but Oberon is getting more and more restless. I wouldn't be surprised if he doesn't wake up here in a day or two."

"Are you headed back to your lab?" asked Carol.

"I am," answered Wally. "I thought I'd go ahead and get the doses ready for in the morning."

"Do you need any help?" asked Carol with a hand on his shoulder.

"No. I'll just be a minute. I wouldn't mind a piece of that cherry pie, though," said Wally.

"Cherry pie," I piped in. "We didn't have any cherry pie with dinner."

Carol tipped her head at Wally and said, "That's your fault. Now you have to share."

"It's my birthday," Wally told me. "Carol made me a cherry pie, but I'll share it with you if you want. You're not hungry, are you?"

Carol didn't wait for me to answer. She faked a couple of laughs and opened the kitchen door. "I'll fix two pieces."

"And I'll get out the vanilla ice cream," I offered before holding out my fist and saying, "Happy birthday."

Bumping fists with me, Wally confessed, "It's not really my birthday. Carol just makes me a birthday pie every now and then because when we were first married, she made me a huge gourmet meal on my birthday and all I said when it was over was, 'What about the cherry pie?' My mother used to make a cherry pie for my birthday, and I just assumed she'd have told Carol about it."

"But she didn't," I guessed.

"No, she did. But Carol didn't want to just keep doing what my mother did. So now I get cherry pie every other month, but never on my real birthday." He laughed, "And with my first bite she always whispers, 'Mama's boy,' in my ear."

Heading back into the house while he rolled himself across the yard, my plan was to hassle Carol for hassling him. But Carol wasn't in the kitchen. I hadn't gotten halfway across the kitchen before I heard Wally scream.

I was the first one to get to the back door, but Maggie was right behind me and pulled me backward as she lunged through the door. "Stay there," she ordered.

Disobeying Maggie at that moment never occurred to me as I watched the horrifying scene through the screen door. Wally's wheelchair was turned over, and he was sprawled out next to it on his belly. There were three hyenas surrounding Wally. One was tugging at his pant legs. The other two were frantically trying to turn him over with a digging-like action. It didn't look like they were trying to hurt him so much as they were trying to get at what he was holding, which we couldn't see because he was lying on it. I assume it was his box of medicine.

Maggie, who had changed from her work clothes into a loose dress, had shed the dress in one quick motion and was charging at the skirmish in her black panther form. It would all be over momentarily, or so I believed until Maggie got hit from the side by a hyena that had been waiting in the shadows. Maggie's attacker hit her in the rib cage with a head butt that knocked the wind out of her and flipped her over on her back.

Before Maggie could right herself, another three hyenas were on her. They had been in the shadows with the head-butter. It was clear, unlike Wally's attackers, Maggie's meant to hurt her or worse. They tore at her with their teeth, trying to keep her on her back where she was most vulnerable and could do the least damage herself.

"No!" I screamed, opening the door. I took a glance around looking for something to swing. For a second I actually thought how nice it would be if there were a sword or two leaning against the doorframe. I settled on Mom's old walking stick.

As I swung the walking stick up over my head and took my first step toward charging into the melee, I felt a giant hand pull me back. It was Oberon. He looked like he just woke up, which was sort of true, and he was buck naked, which was more than a little unnerving. He didn't say a word to me, nor did he look me in the eye. His focus was on joining the fight, which he did with a slow, steady pace. The hyenas didn't seem to notice him until he took hold of one on top of Maggie.

Oberon merely grabbed a handful of flesh between the hyena's front legs and lifted it up and off of Maggie. What happened next is still a mystery to me. When Oberon lifted that hyena he was a man, but as he leaned to toss that foul beast to the side, he became a bear—a massive, blackish-brown grizzly bear.

Up until that moment, Oberon had been silent. But as soon as he tossed that hyena to the side and was all the way into his grizzly bear self, he spread his arms and roared. It was a roar like a roar I had never heard. I do not speak bear, but I know what he said to those hyenas: "I'm here now, you bugs. Flee or die."

And that is what happened. Oberon's roar drew the attention of Aayma's dogs. One by one they threw themselves at him, and one by one he swatted them away like he was killing Japanese beetles with a Ping-Pong paddle.

CHAPTER 35

"FINE"

AIDEN ALLOWED THE PACK TO PURSUE the hyenas across the pasture, "But not deep into the wood." When the pack returned, we did a head count. Twenty-two had been on the chase, but only twenty returned. Two had fallen and were now sleeping with their families. That is how Aiden and the pack referred to the deceased: "sleeping with their families."

Aiden sent a group of five wolves out to run the perimeter and told the remainder of the pack to rest. Then Aiden and Maire took on their human shapes and began a conference with Aunt Maggie and Oberon, who were also again in their human forms. Their conference was in the middle of the yard, the paved space behind the house but within the circle of outbuildings.

Carol, Wally, and I were in the kitchen. While Carol inspected Wally's injuries I watched the conference through the back door. I couldn't hear anything that was being said, but I could tell that Maggie was explaining to Aiden what Oberon had done. Oberon, the only one of the four who was still naked, had his back to me, so I couldn't tell if he had anything to say. Then Oberon bowed his head and turned toward the house. As he made his way inside, the conversation shifted, and it was mostly Aiden who spoke while Maire and Maggie listened and nodded. They looked serious.

Oberon opened the back door, and I really think he would have walked straight through the kitchen without speaking to any of us had Carol not said, "Thank you for saving my husband."

"Fine," said Oberon.

"Yes," said Wally, "thank you. We weren't going to make it without your help."

"Fine," repeated Oberon awkwardly. He was looking straight at Carol and Wally when he spoke, but he looked down when he wasn't speaking. He wasn't blushing anywhere that I could see, but I'd still say he was embarrassed. I don't think any of us was bothered by the fact that he didn't know the proper response to a thank-you. "Fine" was the best he could do, and "fine" was fine with us.

"I should get dressed," Oberon announced.

"Yes," agreed Wally.

As soon as Oberon was gone, Aunt Maggie, Aiden, and Maire entered.

"How is Mr. Wally?" asked Maire.

"I'm fine," declared Wally.

"He won't take off his pants to let me check him out," said Carol.

"I have some scratches from the fall," said Wally. "That's the worst of it. They weren't trying to hurt me. They were trying to get this." He lifted the wooden box on his lap.

Aiden and Maire both nodded at Wally.

"The medicine," said Aiden.

"Smart," said Maire.

"I don't know," observed Wally. "It might have been smarter if they waited until I had replenished the box and then tried to take it."

"It is smart for them," said Maggie. "They are vile and stupid creatures."

"Maybe," said Aiden. "It would have been smarter to have killed you."

We all looked at Wally. He was staring wide-eyed back at Aiden.

"You are the one who can make the medicine. If you die, we have no medicine and the Mother is more in danger."

"Stupid or not," added Maire, "we cannot underestimate them. We lost brothers, and several more have wounds."

"I think Oberon killed that many himself," I said. "He was a machine."

"He was a machine," said Aiden. "And it is a good thing as well, because they must think differently about how to attack him." He held a finger out at us and added, "But they will. It will buy us peace for the rest of the night."

"We hope," interjected Maire.

"We hope," repeated Aiden. "We will keep our eyes on the boundary through the night, just to be safe, but we will probably be safe until tomorrow night."

"And tomorrow?" asked Carol.

"Aayma threatened to overrun us, and we think she will try it tomorrow night," said a somber Aunt Maggie.

Carol's knees buckled. She caught herself so that she didn't fall, but the threat rattled her.

The threat rattled me, too. "What can we do?" I asked.

Maggie and Maire both looked at and stepped away from Aiden, giving him center stage to answer.

"You said that when Oberon was better, you could use him to make better medicine for the Mother," began Aiden. "Is that true?"

"It is," answered Wally.

"Then that is the most important task. If the Mother can wake, she can end this quickly. But we need to prepare to hold out for another night against our enemy."

"Aayma will be increasing her strength during the day," Maggie told us. "Without the Mother we must depend on ordinary means to increase our number."

"And that is our task," said Aiden.

"Increasing our number?" asked Carol.

Aiden nodded his head yes.

"How are we supposed to do that?" asked Carol, her voice trembling.

Aiden frowned and looked to Aunt Maggie.

Maggie understood and told Carol, "You must discover your dominion and assert your will over it."

Carol's eyes rolled up. "What about Jasper?"

"I think I can get a handful of wolverines here by tomorrow night," I volunteered.

"When did you develop a dominion over wolverines?" asked an astonished Aunt Maggie.

"They're in Richmond watching out for Riley," I explained.

"That is wonderful, Jazz-barr," praised Aiden. "But in the morning you could also send out a call for any other wolf packs in the area." To Maggie he added, "We are Jazz-barr's dominion. Wolves, not wolverines. Wolverines are the Mother's."

"What is your dominion, Carol?" asked Maire.

Carol's forehead knotted as she looked back at Maire.

CHAPTER 36

JASPER'S GUESS

WHILE WALLY WENT TO TAKE BLOOD from Oberon, Carol and I went to sit with our mom. When we got there, Mom was still, but she did not have a fever and the color in her face was warmer.

"She's getting better," I said, standing next to her head.

Carol didn't respond. Maybe she didn't hear me. She was busy fluffing pillows and tucking in covers. It was work that didn't need doing, but she apparently needed to be doing something.

"Tell me something, Jasper," she began without looking up right away.

I waited for her to either continue or look at me.

Placing her hands on the bed she leaned forward and looked up at me. "How did you develop your domination over the wolves?"

"Dominion," I corrected her. Then I added, "That's a switch."

"What?"

"Me correcting you," I snorted. "It's weird for me to correct anyone, but I've heard that word, 'dominion,' over and over in the last few days."

"Okay, 'dominion,'" she said, standing up and folding her arms. "How did you develop your dominion?"

"I didn't. I discovered it by accident. What it means and what I'm supposed to do about it are still mysteries to me, but Aiden is teaching me."

"But for you, it's wolves, right?"

I nodded yes.

"So did you pick them, or did they pick you?"

It was a good question and it really stumped me until I realized that she had given me two choices. I was struggling because I assumed one of them had to be true. "Neither, I think," I finally concluded. "I think I was made to be connected to the wolves."

"Made? Made by who?"

"The Creator," I told her.

She looked a bit cross. "So you think we were destined to this?"

I shrugged. "I don't know how it works, but yes, I suppose I do. I don't know if we were destined to have this conversation or if you were destined to make a cherry pie today, but there are things that I think we are destined for. You don't think being Mother Nature's kids was just luck of the draw, do you?"

"I don't know," said Carol, shaking her head. "But right now I wouldn't call it luck either."

I watched her look over Mom awkwardly before saying, "Carol, can I ask you a question?"

"Of course," Carol answered unenthusiastically after a moment of hesitation.

"Do you really have no idea about your dominion? I mean, it seems like you'd have an idea about it."

"Well, I don't," she bristled.

"Well, I do."

Glaring at me, she said, "What's your idea?"

"I think it's birds," I told her.

She closed her eyes and pressed her lips together.

"Look at the way you react when I say that, Carol. If I were wrong you'd just say, 'It doesn't feel right,' but you act like you're afraid I'm right."

She stared at me.

"I'm right, aren't I?"

"I suppose. What makes you think my dominion is birds?"

"Do you remember when you had that dream about me being attacked by vultures in Richmond?"

"Yes. We've talked about this before."

"I know, but I never told you what I think you need to know."

"Which is?"

"It wasn't a dream."

"What do you mean, 'It wasn't a dream'?"

"It all happened, and it happened just the way you saw it."

Her face contorted. "That's not possible."

I waited and watched her bite at her lower lip again.

"You were in Richmond, and I was here," she declared.

"I know."

"It's not possible," she repeated.

"No, it isn't," I agreed. "And yet we have discovered many things that are true but not possible lately."

"I don't know, Jasper. I just don't know."

"Look, Carol, I was there. I felt it. That vulture was on my back, and it was snatched up." I threw my arm down, closed my hand like a claw, and jerked my arm back up quickly as I said, "It felt like Linus and me grabbing the last biscuit off the table. Whatever it was that saved me came from the sky, so a bird—a big bird—is the best guess."

"And according to you, I saw through its eyes," she said. She wasn't sarcastic at all. She was resigned.

CHAPTER 37

TWO CHICKENS FOR BREAKFAST

"JASPER . . . JASPER . . . IT'S TIME TO GET UP. . . . Jasper . . . Jasper." Aunt Maggie's voice was soft and gentle, but she shook me harder and harder until I woke up.

"Did something happen?" I blurted once I realized I was being woken.

"Nothing new has happened," said Maggie heading for the door. "Aiden is waiting for you downstairs. He wants you to send out the scouts."

"Me? How do I do that?"

She didn't answer.

Aiden was waiting for me in the kitchen when I got downstairs. "Jazz-barr, you are rested, I hope."

"I am," I said, "but I don't know what to do."

He smiled. "They know what to do. It is daybreak now. They will go in different directions searching for other wolf packs, and they will begin their return by mid-afternoon in order to be here by evening. They must go in your name if they are to get wolves from other packs to return with them."

"How do I get them to go in my name?" I asked. I was so confused.

Aiden looked at Aunt Maggie for help.

"I think you stand before them and say, 'Go in my name,'" answered Maggie. She looked at Aiden for confirmation.

Aiden nodded yes and said, "There are no special words or ways of speaking. There is just saying it or not. The important thing is that you mean what you say."

That sounded like the kind of advice that would be very handy someday, but it was not today.

I followed him outside where three wolves were lounging on the porch. When we got there the wolves gathered around us.

Remembering what Aunt Maggie told me, I said, "I hope you are successful in what you are about to do. And I hope you return to us safely. Now, go in my name."

The three wolves turned their attention to Aiden. When he said, "Go," they sprinted away.

To me Aiden said, "You see? You were fine. Now, excuse me."

I watched as he trotted over to Carol's house, where Wally was emerging through the front door. I had no particular place to go, so I followed him.

Wally was beaming. "Gentlemen," he called us. "I believe we have it. Oberon was a perfect subject, and his blood was a dream to work with." He was rolling steadily from his house to ours, and then he stopped suddenly and looked at Aiden. "Say, why did you come running over when I came out? Did my wife put you up to that?"

"Yes," answered Aiden. "You were targeted right here last night, so there will always be one of us here when you come and go."

"I don't want special treatment," said Wally.

"That is fine," replied Aiden.

Wally started rolling again, a bit slower this time. "Are you saying, 'Fine, no more special treatment,' or 'Fine, you don't want special treatment'?"

"It was a decision we made without you," answered Aiden.

"Fine," snorted Wally. "Jasper, you're in charge. Tell him no more special treatment."

"I don't really think I'm in charge," I said. The thought of me being in charge scared me a little. "But it seems to me that if you're singled out for attack, then you need special defense whether you want it or not."

Aiden grinned and gently bumped me with his hip as we followed Wally to the house. As I reached for the door Aiden said, "It's time for me to get some sleep. Make sure one of us is with you if you go anywhere."

"Me? Why me?"

"Was your attack random or were to specifically targeted?" he asked. He didn't wait for an answer. Instead he headed to the barn where the pack slept.

That was the moment Carol came outside yawning.

"Were you with Mom?" I asked.

She nodded yes.

"Is she okay?"

"Yes. I just woke up and couldn't get back to sleep, so I came over and sat with her."

"I'm just the opposite. With all that's going on I've been having trouble going to sleep, but once I'm asleep I'm gone. How about you. Do you go to sleep okay?"

"Not lately," said Carol. "I'm actually more like you, except when a dream wakes me up." She shook her head and rubbed her eyes. "I had a psychology professor who told us that when you wake from a recurring dream it means you made a decision, but I can't think of what I'm deciding."

"A 'recurring dream,'" I repeated. "Does that mean you have the same dream over and over?"

"Not the same exactly, but similar dreams. In mine it's like

I'm way up on a cloud surveying the earth below and then I fall." She shuddered. "That's when I wake up."

I started to say something, but she cut me off. "I know, it's only a dream."

"That's not what I was going to say," I told her. "Doesn't that dream remind you of something?"

She eyed me with one eye.

"I think you might have been seeing the world through a bird's eyes and then when it dove down for something you thought you were falling."

"I can't say I'm surprised that you think that. Wally agrees with you, but I don't know. I'm wondering if my dominion is bears."

"Really?"

"Yes. He was outside watching over us when I woke up at three o'clock this morning. Then he came with me to Mom's room. Jasper, he doesn't know who she is. That means she didn't bring him here." Carol shrugged. "Maybe he came here for me. I remembered that you were going to send the wolves out for more wolves, so I thought I'd send him out for more bears."

The picture of an army of Oberons popped in my head. It was exciting. "I think you should."

She frowned. "I already did. He's a grizzly. There are no grizzlies in Appalachia for him to go get, but he would have. He would have done it."

"You know," I said, "just because you have a connection to Oberon doesn't mean you don't have one to birds."

Carol's phone buzzed. She read the screen. "I've got to help Wally give Mom her shot. You need to help Maggie with breakfast."

"Since when does Maggie need help with breakfast?" I asked.

Carol laughed. "Since Oberon ordered two chickens."

CHAPTER 38

RILEY MEETS HER BODYGUARD

RILEY WAS IN HER FRENCH CLASS when I texted, "Call me as soon as you can."

Ten minutes later my phone rang. "Are you okay?" whispered Riley.

"Where are you?" I asked instead of answering.

"I'm in the bathroom," she told me. She sounded annoyed.

"Do you remember Rose?" I asked.

Sounding even more annoyed, Riley said, "Of course I do. Did you get me out of class to ask me that?"

"Look," I said, "I can't explain now, but I really need your help."

"What can I do?"

"I need you to go outside and walk down the sidewalk in front of your school."

"Right," she said. It was the first time I had ever heard her sound sarcastic.

"Really. And once you get close to the corner turn around quickly and see if anyone who looks like a male version of Rose is following you."

She didn't say anything to that.

"It might be one guy or it might be a carload, but don't be afraid. They're your bodyguards."

" 'Don't be afraid,' " she repeated.

"Really, they're there to protect you. They work for my mom." I didn't know for sure that they worked for my mom, but there was no other explanation.

"Was Rose a bodyguard?" asked Riley.

"Yes, she was, and the guy following you is Byron, her brother."

I could hear a door open and close. Then I just listened to squeaky footsteps on a tile floor in an empty hallway. When the squeaks stopped and another door was opened and closed Riley said, "Okay, I'm outside. So this Brian guy is my bodyguard."

"That's 'Byron,' and yes, he's a bodyguard, but he doesn't look like one. He's got blue hair and he's kinda small and he sounds like he's from Kentucky. But he's armed to the teeth and he's tough as nails."

"Like Rose," she observed.

"Like Rose," I agreed.

"What kind of car am I looking for, Jasper?"

"A Mini Cooper," I told her.

"Wait a minute," she said.

I heard more footsteps. No squeaks this time, but I could tell she was jogging. Then I heard her tap on a window.

"Hey," I heard a guy say. The Kentucky accent was missing. "We don't need any Girl Scout cookies, if that's what you want to know."

"I'm Marco," said another guy.

"Well, Marco," said Riley. "I'm looking for Bryon. Vernalisa's son, Jasper, needs to talk to him right away."

In a voice that was farther away from the phone, I heard Byron's voice. "Hand me the phone, darlin'."

"Well, son," said Byron into Riley's phone. "I guess you have a good reason to blow our cover."

"I do," I said. I proceeded to explain to him what we were facing and why I wanted him to come to Boone with as many of his friends as he could muster.

When I was done he said, "I'm not sure I can do that."

"Why not?" I asked.

"Well, for one thing, we already have an assignment." He hesitated. In my mind's eye I pictured him looking at Riley through the window. He asked me, "Does your girlfriend know who we are?"

I could hear Riley answer him. "Bodyguards," she snarled. I could tell she was irritated at him asking me about her with her standing right there next to him.

"That's all she knows," I explained. "What do we need to do to get your team here?"

"I'll have Rose call you," he said.

"Thanks, Byron," I said. "Could you tell me whose dominion you are under?"

With all the talk about Carol's and my dominions I was curious about how he saw it.

"What are you talking about?" asked Riley.

Apparently Bryon finished with our conversation before I did. "I thought I was still talking to Byron," I said.

"Jasper, what's going on?" she asked. Her voice was soft and solemn, which made it harder to lie to her.

"There are things that are going on that I cannot explain right now," I said.

"Cannot or will not?" she asked.

"Some of both," I answered. "But I can tell you that I think, I hope, this will all be over in a couple of days."

"Do you mean your mom getting better or the threats coming to an end?"

"All of the above and more," I said.

"But you can't explain, can you?"

"Not yet, Riley, but soon. I promise." I meant that, too, but as soon as I promised I realized that I had no idea what I could share with her and what I could not. Being part of Mother Nature's family didn't exactly come with an instruction book.

"I have to go," said Riley in a quicker pace. "There's a security guard coming toward me."

CHAPTER 39

TOO SCARED TO FEEL

THE REST OF THE DAY WAS SPENT WAITING. That's the best way to describe how the day went. We waited. Oberon slept all day. He was still camped in Aunt Maggie's room, but I couldn't see that lasting much longer, now that he was awake. Most of the wolves slept, too. There was always one wolf that would appear from nowhere if one of us went outside. And then there was Mom. Mom was definitely doing better. She didn't wake, but she started moving more, especially licking her lips.

Rose never called me, but she sent a text telling me that her brothers would "head to Boone by noon." That would put them here about six o'clock, which was well before dark.

By three o'clock I had developed a better understanding of the term "stir-crazy." I tried to read from my history book, but by the time I'd get to the bottom of the page I couldn't remember what was at the top. *Call of Duty* couldn't hold my interest, and neither could any of the movies I tried.

By 3:30 I was sitting on the back porch watching the grass grow and hoping something would happen. Something did. It was Harlan.

She parked her Blazer on the grass in front of Wally's lab and strolled over toward me. "What's up, Jasper?"

"Nothing," I said, using my standard answer in spite of the truth.

Harlan stopped directly in front of me. With her hands on her hips and her head tipped forward enough to be looking at me over her glasses, if she were wearing glasses, she went into schoolteacher scolding mode. "What's up with you not telling anyone you were back?"

"Ah . . . ," was the best answer I could come up with.

"Good answer," she smirked.

"I just got home yesterday," I defended myself in a whiny voice.

She sat down next to me. "So you're not staying in Richmond?"

"No," I told her. "How did you know that?"

We both answered, "Riley," at the same time.

"Did something happen?" she asked.

I looked at her to see if I could read her face. I thought she looked worried.

"Nothing happened in Richmond," I assured her. "Riley and I are fine. I came back because my mom's been sick and she started getting better." It was sort of true and it made sense to me when I said it.

It didn't look like it made sense to Harlan, though, but she didn't ask me why I had gone away when my mother was sick in the first place.

Eventually she nodded a few times and stood back up. "Well, your girlfriend just asked me to check on you, so that's what I'm doing. Right now I'm headed to work, but let's have coffee this weekend."

"Sounds good," I said. What I thought was, *I hope I'm alive.* That was the first moment that I was actually aware that I could get killed. My next thought was to note how curious it was that I wasn't scared. I knew I was supposed to be scared. I knew I must be scared, but I guess I was just too scared to feel it.

CHAPTER 40

"MY WAY OR YOURS?"

LATE AFTERNOON CAME and brought a carload of wolverines from Richmond. They weren't in their wolverine forms, but they were unmistakably warriors. The driver and the two from the backseat got out of the car and stretched. Each one had brightly dyed hair and piercings. Each one stood confidently and surveyed the surroundings in a different direction. Byron got out of the passenger side of the car and sauntered over to where Aiden and I were standing in the yard. Byron was as lean as Aiden but not as sharp and angular.

"Y'all need some help?" he asked.

Aiden's nose twitched and then he smiled at me, "Your friends?"

I introduced them. "This is Rose's brother from Richmond." To Byron I added, "Aiden is alpha in the pack."

Byron tipped his head respectfully. "I understand I owe you thanks for pulling Rose out of that place in Hendersonville."

Tipping his head in a smaller bow Aiden said, "Your sister was a valiant servant. The pack would come to her aid as one of our own, as I trust we will come to regard you all."

Byron grinned crookedly. "So when does this party start anyway?"

"Soon enough," answered Oberon with a yawn. He had come outside and was standing close behind us.

"Oberon? Is that you, big fella?" asked Byron. He didn't appear to need an answer as he spread his arms and embraced Oberon. The bigger man didn't bend down but awkwardly patted the smaller man on the back. Byron was clearly enjoying Oberon's discomfort.

"My way or yours?" asked Byron when Oberon let him go.

"He is alpha here," answered Oberon, nodding his head toward Aiden.

"The big fella here and I have never gone to war together, but we have argued about it," explained Byron.

"I see," said Aiden.

"We've had opportunities to fight together, but it's not our way to wait," said Byron. The crooked grin had returned.

Oberon shoved the much smaller man playfully.

"Now, don't let this guy fool you, boys. He's fast. Real fast. But he likes to let the fight come to him." Byron winked. "I think he's lazy."

Oberon shook his head slowly. "I don't understand why the Creator made you reckless *and* little."

Byron laughed. "He doesn't mean 'reckless,' he means fearless and quick." He juked from side to side, saying, "It's better to be quick than fast once you're up close and personal."

"We are glad for your help," said Aiden in a serious tone. "The pack prefers to track its enemy and fight when it is most advantageous to us. That way we minimize our risks."

"But when the time comes, you turn the warriors loose, do you not?" asked Byron.

"Of course," said Oberon. "That would be true for all of us. Our differences are about when to turn the warriors loose."

Aiden nodded his agreement. "As for this fight we are fighting for time." He stared hard at each of the others, including me. "This fight is over when the Mother wakes. We are keeping her safe while she rids herself of the mamba poison." He looked toward the house, "The Mother could wake tonight."

CHAPTER 41

TWO SPARTANS

AT DUSK AIDEN AND OBERON STOOD side by side on the near side of the pasture directly behind our compound. From their position the pasture sloped gently down to the back fence. Beyond that fence was the back pasture, which sloped upward to the woods beyond. Any attack from Aayma and her minions would come from that direction.

The position that Aiden and Oberon held was a deliberately defiant one. It wasn't intended to frighten them, for it wasn't a show of force. We didn't want her to know what kind of force we had mustered because we were fairly sure it would not have scared her in the least.

Earlier we had had a conversation in the kitchen about how the evening would begin. Carol started it off with the suggestion, "Why don't we all line up across the back and show Aayma how strong we are? That should give her second thoughts about an attack."

"We cannot scare her," Aiden told us. "She cares not how many she loses."

"We must crush her," Oberon answered Aiden.

"We'll do it," Byron chimed in.

"You cannot kill the Mother's daughter," Aunt Maggie told Byron.

Byron exhaled loudly. "Y'all sure make this hard."

"Protecting the Mother is our responsibility," Aiden said crisply. He scanned the circle slowly. "It is our only responsibility. We will do nothing that detracts from this responsibility in the slightest. Agreed?"

Looking at Aiden's eyes, I could not imagine anyone not agreeing with him at that moment. No one disagreed, but Byron took hold of Aiden's hand and said, "For the Mother's sake, we will submit to your authority, but I beg you. No, I insist that, should the moment arise that we could be loosed to go for Aayma, you give us leave to finish this once and for all."

"You are no match for her," Aunt Maggie told him.

Byron went to the back door and yelled to his men, "Say, boys, we are no match for taking out their leader. Anybody wanna go back home?"

The answers were "Nope," "Not me," and "Are you kidding?"

Then Byron asked, "If we get the chance, shall we go for her even though we're no match for her?"

Again they answered as he expected: "I'm in," "Of course," and finally a "That's what we do," which was then echoed by the other two.

Byron strolled back to where the group stood. Looking at Aiden he asked,

"Do you agree?"

Aiden looked first at him and then at Maggie. "Aayma will flee before she is harmed." Turning back to Byron he said, "Agreed."

"The most you could accomplish is to make her flee, for she is a coward at heart," added Aunt Maggie.

Byron's grin got bigger. "I expect that'd do, wouldn't it?"

And so it was agreed: we weren't really trying to win, but we were defensively buying time for my mother to recover and make things right. There was no doubt in anyone's mind that she could do that—at least no doubt was in my mind, nor was any doubt uttered. The concern was if Wally's antidote would work and would it work in time.

So, in the meantime, there they stood: Aiden and Oberon side by side in the pasture like two Spartans waiting for the Immortals to show up.

CHAPTER 42

JASPER GOES UP TOP

WALLY, BY VIRTUE OF HIS WHEELCHAIR and as developer of the antidote, was to stay inside tending to Mom. Carol and I were relegated to staying inside as well. I, by virtue of the wolves being my dominion, was told to stay clear of the fighting but within eyesight of it. The wolves were my dominion, and although I still had no idea what that truly meant, I did know that at that very moment the least I could do was offer my support and encouragement.

Carol and Wally were in Mom's room when I peeked in.

"Where is everybody?" asked Wally.

"Aiden and Oberon are out on the lawn, and everyone else is waiting in the shadows to join them when the time comes," I answered.

"So it's just us humans inside right now," said Carol.

It was said with a smile, so I'm pretty sure she was trying to be funny or brave. Either way it didn't work, because her voice cracked when she spoke and her smile looked as though it came off a Halloween mask.

"How's Mom?" I asked. It was the question I intended to ask when I entered, but now it had the added benefit of changing the subject.

They both glanced at Mom, Wally from the end of the bed and Carol sitting on the bed's edge. I stepped closer and looked down. She definitely appeared better. For the first time in days and days she looked more like she was asleep than unconscious. Her skin looked natural, and she wasn't hot when I put my hand on her head.

I kept my hand there as I looked at Wally. "When does she get the next shot?"

Looking at his watch he said, "In about an hour."

I looked at Carol. "That will do it. I feel it in my bones."

Carol stood abruptly and trotted around me and out the bedroom door. She was hunched over slightly and covering her face with her hands.

"Carol?" I pleaded as she went by, but she didn't respond.

When she was gone I sat down in the place she left next to Mom. "Did I say something wrong?" I asked Wally.

"No, Jasper, it wasn't what you said. It's—" he rubbed the top of his head and then his face. "It's everything." Sitting up straighter he said, "You know your sister. She's the most put-together person I know. I've never seen anything rattle her like this has. I don't think she's ever been afraid before."

"This has everyone rattled," I said. "We're all afraid." I pointed toward the pasture. "I think this even has Aunt Maggie a little off."

"I know," he said. "You're right, but there's more. As scary as all this is, it at least makes sense."

We stared at each other for a moment before I asked, "Did you actually say this makes sense?"

We both laughed. We laughed hard. Right before a battle was a weird time to laugh, but that's what we were doing. I'm sure I was dumping a lot of pent-up fear and confusion into my laughter, because I definitely felt lighter when we were done.

"I know," Wally said, rubbing his eyes. "I can't believe I said that either, but it's true. Once I accepted the fact that I'm married to Mother Nature's daughter and we live with a black panther housekeeper, then the rest of this does make sense." Extending an open hand toward me, he added, "Doesn't it?"

It did. I nodded yes.

"But in addition to all of this, Carol's been having what we used to think were nightmares, but now they seem like something else." He pointed out the window. "There are premonitions or visions about things that happen. Remember when Oberon was attacked? She had a vision about that." Then his eyebrows went up. "Yeah, and what about that thing that happened to you on the way back from Richmond? Was that a premonition?"

He stopped. He was breathing hard and staring at me, but I didn't think he was waiting for an answer.

"No," I said.

" 'No,' " he repeated with a confused look on his face. "No, what?"

"No, it wasn't a premonition," I answered.

"What are you two talking about?" asked Carol from the door.

I left it to Wally to answer that question. Instead I stood and offered her seat back to her.

"That's okay," she told me. "You can sit there."

I shook my head no and said, "I'm not staying."

Carol put her hands on her hips and stepped directly in my way. "Where do you think you're going?"

Clearly the take-charge Carol had returned.

I opened my mouth, but before I could answer she put her finger against my chest and told me, "You're not going out there."

I put my hands up. "I'm not going out there. I'm going up top to the observation deck."

"Why?" she asked. Her voice was breathy and seemed to deflate her as she asked.

"I don't know," I shrugged. "I know I have some kind of power or influence with the wolves."

"Maybe so," she admitted, "but how are you going to use it up there?"

I snorted. "I don't know. I just know it's something I can do. If my being there doesn't matter, then it won't hurt that I'm up there. But if my being there mattered, and I don't understand how it could, then it might help."

She looked at Wally.

"He's right," said Wally.

"You should come up with me," I told her. I hadn't planned on suggesting that, but at that moment it seemed like the right thing to say.

Carol recoiled a little. "I don't see how my being there would help anything, Jasper."

I held out an open palm to her. "It couldn't hurt."

She looked at Wally.

"I've got your mom," he told her.

They stared at each other, and then she slowly lifted her hand. All three of us watched her hand make its way into mine. Just before she took hold of me, she looked at Wally again. He closed his eyes and nodded yes as her hand landed in mine.

We were both quiet as I led her down the hall and up the flight of stairs to the observation deck. The sky was clear as I opened the door. Cool night air rushed in toward us right away. Just as I stepped forward to the roof, Carol's hand jerked from my grip. It happened so fast that my reaction was to look at my empty hand to see if hers was still there. It wasn't.

"I just can't," was all she said as she descended the stairs two at a time.

CHAPTER 43

TWO EQUALS TWELVE

I WATCHED, BUT I DIDN'T SAY ANYTHING. It didn't even occur to me to call out to Carol as she fled. There was nothing to flee, but she was fleeing. I watched as she exited the door at the bottom of the stairs without looking back up at me. Then I stood there watching the empty staircase well beyond the *click* sound declaring the closing of the door.

What I noticed next was what I wasn't noticing. There were none of the usual evening or night sounds, the sounds that don't sound like sounds until you don't hear them anymore. The silence was eerie.

Walking over to the railing I looked out over the pasture. There was no sign of Aayma or her minions, but even from where I watched I could tell that both Aiden and Oberon were at full alert. Even though they were facing away from me, I could tell they were sensing something.

"Is it happening?" whispered a voice next to me.

Lurching forward in a dry-heave sort of convulsion, I could feel my organs rearrange themselves and my eyeballs try to escape. I was lucky I didn't throw myself off the roof. At least I didn't yell. It was Aunt Maggie. I hadn't heard her come up the stairs.

"What are you doing here?" I asked when my throat cleared. "I thought you were down there."

"I was," she whispered. "But the bear thought I should be in here just in case your sister sends one of her vermin around behind us."

"I wish you wouldn't call her that," I snapped quietly.

I stared at her trying to will her to look back at me, but her focus was straight ahead. When I finally gave up and followed her gaze across the pasture I could see Aayma. She was just in view on the open side of the line of trees beyond the back pasture. She didn't seem to notice Aiden or Oberon at all. All she was tending to were the dozen hyenas that surrounded her like a pack of pups. It was a playful scene, with Aayma nurturing her dogs and them responding to her scratching their ears and rubbing their bellies like they were beloved pets, but all I felt at the time was loathing. I hated everything about those creatures. How I felt about her was beyond my ability to describe.

I must have been sneering as I watched them, because the right side of my upper lip began to ache and I had to turn away and exercise my lips. As I turned I noticed the same thing happening to Aunt Maggie. Only for her it was her hands. She was gripping the edge of the railing around the observation deck so tightly that the knuckles on her very black hand were turning very pink.

"You're hurting your hand," I told her, putting my hands on top of hers.

She shook her head as if she was waking from a trance. "Oh, my," she exhaled loudly, moving her hands around to get the blood flowing back in them.

At first I thought Maggie was referring to her hands as she shook them, but she was still staring across the pasture. When I looked, "Oh, my," came out of my mouth, too.

Aayma was moving. She was crossing the field with her dogs spread out behind her. At that point Aayma was about as far from the back gate as Aiden and Oberon were in the pasture. They were all approaching that back gate at the same pace. Everyone would get there at the same time.

"She just wants to talk," observed Maggie.

It was a strange thing to say. I had thought Aayma progressed from interfering with our search for cures, to taking more dominion for herself, and finally to the utter destruction of my mother's position as Mother Nature. She was bringing her soldiers as she marched toward us. She didn't look to me like she just wanted to talk, so I asked, "How can you tell?"

Maggie nodded in the direction of the gate. "She is only bringing enough with her to equal what she faces."

"They have us outnumbered twelve to two," I blurted.

"Those two more than equal her twelve," said Maggie without a hint of emotion. She was simply stating a fact.

We watched as both sides reached the back gate. Each group stayed on its side of the fence. Maggie and I couldn't hear what was being said, but as expected, Aayma was doing all the talking. As she talked she paced casually back and forth in front of her dogs, occasionally pointing toward the house or at the woods behind her. Every now and then the hyenas would bark and posture as if they were ready to charge the gate. If Aiden or Oberon was reacting to anything she was saying, I couldn't tell from behind.

The conversation, which looked more like a lecture, went on for ten minutes before Aayma seemed to take note of the antics of her entourage. By then they were no longer barking their occasional support for something she was saying, but the hyenas had progressed to a steady desire to challenge Aiden and Oberon.

They were all gathered together, crouching and snarling, poised to attack.

We watched Aayma turn to them. Her right arm swept across the space above them, and they shrank down, watching her hand. It looked like she was scolding them as they cowered.

"Worthless creatures," muttered Maggie.

Then Maggie and I both gasped. Two of those worthless creatures broke free from the pack and charged through the gate. They both attacked Oberon rather than splitting up. The first one through the gate leaped very high. He would have landed on Oberon's back had Oberon remained on all fours—but he didn't. Instead he reared up on his hind legs and swatted the leaping hyena back across the fence. It all happened very fast. Oberon looked like a volleyball player spiking the vermin over the net.

The second hyena came at Oberon low, taking advantage of the bear's exposed lower body. From our vantage point we couldn't tell if the attack reached Oberon, but the hyena could not have done much damage because Aiden was on top of him in a flash. Oberon dropped back down to all fours and moved, giving us a clear view of Aiden over the top of the squirming hyena. Aiden's jaws were clamped down on his victim's neck.

The remaining hyenas rushed to the gate, but they didn't cross through it. Oberon had moved to a position so near the gate that had they attempted to cross the gate it would have had to be one at a time. Oberon would have easily picked each of them off.

When it was clear they weren't coming, Oberon sat back and roared directly at them. Even from that distance I could see his left lip flap in the force of his roar.

As the hyenas slinked in response, Aayma waved her hand in dismissal and began to make her way back to the woods she came from. Her minions followed her. The one in Aiden's mouth had stopped squirming and was lying spread-eagle in surrender. Aiden gave him a last shake and let him go. Aiden and Oberon watched him as he crept by them and through the gate.

None of them even glanced at the one Oberon had swatted across the fence.

CHAPTER 44

AIDEN'S TEARS

"IT WILL BE SOON," SAID MAGGIE SOFTLY. Again she spoke without emotion. She said it with neither satisfaction nor fear. It was simply an observation. She spoke and then she was gone.

I didn't notice when she left. My concentration was fixed upon Aiden and Oberon as they returned to the near side of the pasture where a few wolves waited for them. As soon as they reached the near gate, Aiden was surrounded by his pack. Their conference didn't last long before more wolves joined them. I don't know how they were communicating, but I know they were communicating because all of them, at the exact same time, stopped suddenly and looked up to where I watched from the observation deck on the roof. It startled me. Clearly they expected something, but all I had to offer was my respect and appreciation. I nodded. It was the only thing I could think of to do.

At that the wolves sprang back into action, half taking a line to the left flank and the other half to the right. One wolf—Maire, I think—stayed in the middle with Aiden. I felt a little bad that they gave me so much power, while I still had a hard time recognizing each of them in their wolf form.

For his part, Oberon simply turned around and sat when he and Aiden had returned from their powwow with Aayma.

"I hate this."

It was Carol. She was standing behind me with her arms folded around her middle. It looked like she was cold, but it wasn't cold.

"You came back," I said.

"Aunt Maggie sent me up." She pointed at the field below us with her chin. "She says they need to see us."

I held my left arm open to invite her to step up to the rail where I was standing.

She managed half a step closer. With her arms still folded across her middle, she asked, "Does any of this make sense to you?"

I shook my head no.

"But you seem to handle it better," she said.

That thought made me chuckle once. I'm sure I was too scared for a full-scale laugh.

"Did I say something funny?" she asked harshly.

"I'm sorry," I apologized. "I didn't mean to irritate you. It's just funny. I mean, you're one of the smartest people I know. You make sense out of everything, Carol." I shrugged and shuffled my feet. "As for me, nothing makes sense. I'll bet that half the decisions I've ever made were made without making sense of what I was facing. Not complete sense anyway."

She shook her head. "I don't want to blame Mom for all of this, especially with her like she is, but geez, what has she gotten us into?"

"I know," I said, turning back to the rail. I looked across the field, where I could see hyenas emerging from the woods. I began to count, just to compare numbers, but the way they kept moving in and out of the shadows made counting impossible.

"You know," I said as I watched, "if you need someone to blame for all of this, I'd say Aayma is a better choice than Mom."

"Yes, absolutely, but Mom should have prepared us better," Carol huffed. "She didn't prepare us at all."

"You don't know that, Carol."

She gave me one of those you're-out-of-your-mind looks.

"Well, you don't," I continued. "You said it yourself: This doesn't make sense. So you probably don't know what you need now, and if you don't know that, then you don't know if you are prepared or not."

Pointing across the field Carol said, "Maybe not, but I know I'm not prepared for that."

There were now maybe forty or fifty hyenas in the back pasture. They were just milling around, occasionally looking in the direction of the house. Aayma was nowhere in sight, but she was surely watching from somewhere in the shadows.

"What is that?" I heard myself ask out loud. A large albino hyena strolled out of the woods. He was significantly larger than the other hyenas, who seemed to gather around him as he walked slowly across the back field and through the back gate. Just inside the gate he stopped, allowing the other hyenas to pass the gate and spread out on either side of him. His gaze never strayed from Aiden and Oberon.

Maire, Aiden, and Oberon moved forward, taking a position at the crest of a slight incline. Wolves fanned out on either side of them, forming a curve rather than a straight line. The positioning of the two groups made it easy for me to get a good count, which I did pointing with my finger.

"Forty-four for them and twenty-three for us," I told Carol when I was done. "But one of them is *not* equal to one of us," I added, remembering Maggie's words. I was also aware that a black panther and four wolverines were not yet accounted for on the battlefield.

Oberon roared. The wolves howled. And the hyenas yapped

back. The big white hyena in the middle just stared until the chatter slowed down. Then, looking to his right, he nodded, and the entire company of hyenas to his right began coming across the pasture. They weren't sprinting, and they weren't charging straight ahead. They were headed diagonally toward the middle of our line, straight at Maire, Aiden, and Oberon.

As the hyenas looped across the field, black panther Maggie joined the trio in the middle. I watched the hyenas as they shifted into a full-on sprint as they crossed the halfway point. Our foursome squared up to the coming attack as the wolves on either side held their positions.

I pulled my left arm away reflexively before I realized that it was just Carol grabbing hold of my sleeve. She let go right away but then used her hand to point to the back of the pasture.

The hyenas that had not been part of the first charge—the ones to the left of the big white one—had circled around him and were sprinting as hard as they could toward our left flank. From my vantage point it looked like they were going to engage the wolves of the left flank just after the first group hit our middle.

As the first twenty-two hyenas got close, Oberon buried his head and plowed back into them, knocking six of them off stride and backward—and those were the lucky ones. Once he made initial contact with the others, he threw his head up and began swatting at them with his huge paws. He got one with his right, then another with his left, and finally a third with his right again. If they hadn't figured out to steer clear of his paws, he'd have wiped them all out himself.

Maggie took a position on Oberon's right side protecting his flank and her rear. There were four hyenas in a semicircle around her, staying out of reach of her less powerful but faster paws. She had made quick work of the first hyena that squared off with her.

Aiden and Maire stayed on Oberon's left. They, too, were surrounded by hyenas. There weren't any dead lying around them, but they had each mixed it up with two and three hyenas at a time. The wolves didn't have the benefit of long claws, so killing with a single swipe like Oberon, or Maggie to a lesser extent, was not an option for them.

While trying to surround the four from our middle, the hyenas left themselves exposed to rear attacks from the wolves on either side, which is exactly what happened. Three wolves from our left flank and another three from our right threw themselves into the fray. Pouncing, they clamped their powerful jaws on the backs of the necks of their prey. With a couple of violent jerks of their heads, the wolves dispatched another five hyenas with broken necks. A sixth managed to wiggle free when the wolf that clamped on his neck threw him sideways when he jerked his head.

The remaining hyenas in the first assault threw themselves at Maire in an uncoordinated frenzy. They managed to knock her down and tear at her underbelly and hind legs. They were definitely doing some damage. I bit my lip as I watched, and I'm sure I was holding my breath, too.

The strategy of throwing themselves so feverishly at Maire, although harming her, was disastrous for the hyenas, leaving them defenseless as Oberon, Maggie, and a few of the wolves picked them off easily.

In short order, the hyenas from the first attack were all dead, and the only injury I could tell on our side was that Maire had taken a beating and was limping noticeably.

The second attack, which was happening simultaneously next to the first, was a different story. While the first attack drew all our attention, the second attack is where we suffered the most damage. When the first attack ended, all of the wolves joined in on what had been happening on our left flank. The hyenas outnumbered the wolves twenty-two to eight once the attack on the middle drew three away and kept any possible aid distracted.

When the first attack was over, the wolves, Maggie, and Oberon joined the mix of the second attack. Oberon swatted four or five as he waded in, and Maggie added another two to that number. The wolves killed another six, and the few remaining hyenas retreated back across the field.

There were plenty of hyenas lying motionlessly on the field. The remaining ones were leaving the field, so we won. But it was a joyless victory, because there were six wolves from the left flank down and not moving. I didn't know if they were dead or injured. I wasn't going to find out from where I was either.

"I gotta go," I mumbled as I lurched past Carol and down the stairs.

"Don't you go out there," ordered Carol.

That didn't stop me.

What stopped me was Byron and the other wolverines, who were all in human form and stationed in the kitchen. They watched everything through the window.

"Hold on there, cowboy," Byron said to me.

That's not what stopped me either. What really stopped me was the wolverine leaning on the back door.

"I gotta get out there," I virtually begged him.

"We can't do it," said Byron, patting me on the back. "We're in here to keep them out and you in."

"I have to get out there," I pleaded. "It's all over out there. They need me."

"If they need, you they'll come in here to get you. It's not a secret where you are."

All I could do was watch through the back window. Aiden, Maire, Maggie, and Oberon were all in human form by that time.

They were in the middle of the compound talking. I slid the window open so that I could hear them.

Aiden, who had been standing with his back to the house, turned when he heard me open the window.

"Stay there, Jazz-barr," he ordered abruptly. He turned toward me when he yelled, so for just a moment I could see his face. There were tears streaming down his cheek. The sight of him crying caught me completely off guard. I was near tears until that moment. I don't know what I felt after that.

I remembered my brother, Linus, telling me about seeing our father cry for the first time. It was when our grandfather died trying to save his dog that had fallen through some ice. Our father died when I was two, so I don't remember seeing him cry. I do remember when Linus told me that story. We were at a funeral for Mrs. Kincaide, a neighbor. Mr. Kincaide was standing next to the casket, and his kids were watching him. That's when Linus said, "Seeing your dad cry was like living through the moment just before the world ended."

Now I know what he meant.

CHAPTER 45

MALCOLM

"IT ISN'T OVER," MAGGIE TOLD THEM. "That was just to weaken us. She cares nothing for what it costs her. She will continue to weaken us until she thinks she can take what she wants."

"Which is the Mother," said Maire. She was standing awkwardly on her right leg and holding her left side.

No one spoke immediately after that. We all knew how serious this was, but it was still sobering to be reminded.

"How is the Mother now?" asked Maire. She was looking toward my window.

"I don't know."

"Please find out for us," Maire told me.

I stepped away from the window, but I heard something that made me keep listening.

"We need you, Aiden," said Maggie firmly.

"It was my fault." His voice trembled.

"It's war," said Oberon calmly. "There is always death."

"Don't you think I know that?" snapped Aiden. "This is not my first war. And it is not my first death."

"No," said Maire with the same firmness as Maggie's. "It's the first time you've been outsmarted. Is that it?"

I couldn't believe she said that to him. His head jerked toward her. I don't think Aiden believed she'd say that either.

"I was outsmarted," he said. He sounded tired.

Maire shoved him hard, causing him to step back and for her to shift her weight to her left leg. The shift made her cry out and hop on her right leg.

Aiden immediately reached out to steady her.

"You are the alpha," Maire told him.

Keeping his hands on her, he leaned slightly to look toward where the left flank had been attacked. I couldn't see, but I assumed that is where most of the wolves were.

"You see," continued Maire, "you are the alpha. No one is challenging you."

"If mistakes were made, think about them later," barked Maggie. "Right now we need to be ready for whatever is coming, and," she emphasized, pounding her finger on his chest, "you are the alpha."

He looked at Oberon.

"I don't argue with women when they're right," said Oberon.

Aiden nodded, stepped back from their conference, and in an authoritative voice told the pack, "Bring our fallen to the barn. We will honor their lives later. We need to prepare."

Aiden wasn't talking to me when he gave his orders, but I went to check on Mom as if he was.

The news was good. Wally had given her another dose of the antidote. Mom's temperature was normal, and she was sleeping peacefully.

"She's still weak," said Wally, "but she could wake up any moment. I bet she'll be as good as new when she wakes tomorrow morning."

I reported back with Wally's exact phrase.

"Good," said Aiden. "We don't have to win. We just have to get through the night."

Maire and Maggie both nodded their agreement. I couldn't see where Oberon was.

"Byron, can you hear me?" asked Aiden toward the open window.

The wolverines were sitting around our kitchen table.

"Loud and clear, cappy," returned Byron.

"We're going to need you out here," said Aiden.

"Let's go, boys," said Byron.

"They need us," answered one of the wolverines in a singsongy voice.

They all laughed as they headed for the back door.

"Party time," said Byron.

I followed them out.

The entire pack was now in human form, and they were following Aiden's orders for moving bodies. Because of his size and strength Oberon was the only one who was carrying a body by himself. Cradled gently in his arms was Malcolm Cahan. He was alive but badly hurt.

Back when I thought they were all Russian immigrant security guards, Malcolm was the first one in the pack to be nice to me. He was the first to call me Jazz-barr. He was a fierce warrior and one of Aiden's most trusted lieutenants, but he was also the most playful member of the pack.

"Not Malcolm," I yelled when I saw him. I had mistaken him for dead. I immediately regretted yelling, because it made him flinch and then cry out in pain.

When Malcolm flinched, Oberon just lifted him a little higher in his arms, saying, "I'm just moving you where it's safe."

I followed Oberon to the bunkhouse.

Oberon was gentle in a way only his strength would allow. He lay Malcolm on an empty cot and knelt down next to him.

"Do you need anything, brother?" he asked.

"No," said Malcolm weakly. "I will just go to sleep."

"Jasper is here," Oberon informed him.

"Okay."

Oberon stood. He looked at me and nodded ever so slightly. His eyes were glassy. He left us alone.

"Jazz-Barr," Malcolm called to me.

I knelt by Malcolm where Oberon had been. "Jazz-Barr," Malcolm repeated. His voice soft and steady.

I took hold of his left hand, which was lying at his side.

He moved his hand to his stomach and placed his right hand on top of mine. "Don't be afraid. I have to go to sleep now."

I couldn't speak so I gently squeezed his hand.

He squeezed back. He smiled and said, "You'd have been a great wolf." Then he let go.

I couldn't bear to look at him. I knew he didn't have much time left, but I couldn't watch. Lying my arm gently across his middle, I buried my head in the bedding next to him. I listened as his breathing became heavier. He moaned in pain as he struggled to move. As I lifted my face to see if I could help, I could see that he had changed into his natural form. With another strained moan he licked my face and lay his head down.

CHAPTER 46

"IS THAT ALL YOU GOT?"

"JASPER!" SAID AUNT MAGGIE. I'm not sure, but I think it might have been the fourth time she said my name. She was standing in the doorway of the bunkhouse.

I let go of Malcolm's paw and pushed on the edge of the cot until I was standing over him. I looked down at him as if I hadn't been looking at him for the last few minutes. All I could think was, *It isn't him anymore.*

"Now, Jasper!" Maggie was getting frustrated with me. I could hear it in her voice. I just couldn't translate that into action.

"Now," she said softly, taking me by the elbow and leading me from the bunkhouse.

I went with her without thinking about it.

She led me across the compound to the house. "It's time to go inside," she said, nudging me toward the two steps leading to the back door. "Go inside and wash your face."

Slowly I climbed the two steps up to the back deck and turned around. That's when I really woke up. Standing just inside the gate across the pasture were three vultures, like the ones that had attacked us outside of Galileo's, the ones who kidnapped Riley. They were in their human form. I hated them.

"Go!" said Maggie from the ground. "Inside!"

"Go inside!" yelled Aiden from the edge of the pasture.

Maggie raised her eyebrows and nodded her head yes. So inside and up the stairs I went.

By the time I was on the observation deck, Aunt Maggie, Oberon, and the wolves had all returned to their natural form. Only Byron and the wolverines were still in human form.

I watched as they waited patiently. I assumed they were patient. I know I sure wasn't. I had begun pacing back and forth on the roof, but I didn't notice I was pacing until I stopped to watch more of those dorky-looking vultures come out of the forest and cross the far back pasture. I hated the way they walked. One of them looked straight at me and laughed.

"I hobe I ead your face off," I screamed at him from the roof. I knew it sounded stupid as soon as I said it. No one but me seemed to notice I had said anything.

Then Byron turned around and looked up at me. He grinned and tapped the side of his head with the tip of his finger. At first I assumed he agreed with me about how stupid it was, but before he turned back around he gave me a thumbs-up.

There must have been twelve or thirteen vultures all leaning against the back fence when the hyenas began coming out. At first it looked like they outnumbered us slightly. I thought of Aayma somewhere back in the shadows watching and maneuvering her side. I thought, *They're going to need a lot more of them than that if they think they have a chance.*

My confidence was short-lived. Almost as if Aayma had read my thoughts, she sent out another wave of those disgusting dogs. This group was twice the size of the first. The vultures, still just leaning back against the fence, laughed as all the hyenas flowed by.

There was nothing orderly about them. They seemed to flaunt the idea that there were so many of them that strategy didn't matter.

It would matter to Aiden, I thought, looking down at the back of his head. His warriors were all in place, holding their positions as he intended. None of his warriors even glanced in his direction. They were all looking straight across the field at an enemy that could do exactly what Aayma threatened to do: over-run us. They all knew that he knew what they were facing, and they trusted him without thinking about the cost.

I knew I should have been afraid, but I didn't feel it. Maybe I was so afraid that I *couldn't* feel it. I'd been that afraid before, and that turned out okay because Aiden and the pack had showed up.

I took hold of the wolf's-tooth necklace. That's what I had done the first time Aiden and the pack had shown up to save me. There was a time when I believed holding that wolf's tooth magically made the pack appear. Now I held it for comfort.

With the throng of hyenas milling about in a swarm, I hadn't noticed Aayma come out of the forest. By the time I spotted her, she was already inside the back fence with seven of her vultures gathered around her.

Where are the other six? I wondered, and then I saw my answer.

The other six had taken their vulture form and were now taking flight.

"They're coming," I yelled.

Black panther Aunt Maggie turned her head to glance in my direction. Byron gave me a thumbs-up, but he didn't turn.

When my eyes returned to the vultures they were already halfway across the field, and they had what looked like ropes or hoses in their claws.

"Black mambas, black mambas!" I screamed, leaning as far over the rail as I could.

All I got back this time was another thumbs-up from Byron.

They're ready, I told myself as I leaned back from the rail and took hold of the wolf's tooth again.

As the vultures neared our side of the field, Byron and the wolverines stopped leaning on the fence and took positions behind where Aiden and the center group were. It was clear from my angle that the wolverines were lining themselves up with where the vultures were targeting, which was either Aiden himself or Aiden and the entire center group.

When the vultures dipped down, the wolverines moved in between Maire, Aiden, Oberon, and Maggie. The first two snakes were dropped toward Aiden. Byron caught one in his bare hands and quickly broke its neck. I almost laughed. It looked about as easy for him to do as it is for me to snag one of Maggie's biscuits from the table.

I didn't laugh, though, because the second snake, also aimed at Aiden, was caught by the wolverine on the other side of our alpha. This catch was not as skillful as Byron's had been. This time the snake was still caught in midair, but just not behind the head as Byron had done. This snake was snared in the middle, allowing the head to swing around and latch onto the bare arm of the wolverine that caught it.

"No!" I gasped.

The wolverine flinched, and with his other hand he pinched the snake just behind the head. He turned in my direction. I could see him grit his teeth as he squeezed the snake until it went limp. Then he pried the jaw open and threw the dead snake over the fence.

I watched in amazement as the wolverine put his arm to his mouth and sucked on the wound. I remembered how quickly Benjamin had died after being bit in Hendersonville. I discovered later that black mamba venom didn't affect wolverines the way it did humans, but at that moment I thought maybe they had all gotten immunization shots from Wally. It was the puncture and not the poison that seemed to bother the wolverine. I kept watching as he spit and turned back to the action.

The other four snakes were dropped on the ground in front of the center group. The air attack hadn't worked at all. All four snakes made it to the ground, but the other two wolverines picked up two of them immediately and made very quick work of it. They made killing the poisonous snakes look about as difficult as taking the lid off a mayonnaise jar.

Another snake was making its way toward Maire and ended up in Aiden's jaws. I'm pretty sure it was Aiden's bite that did it in, but just to be sure, Aiden violently shook his head back and forth, making the snake's body flop around like a whip. It looked limp to me long before Aiden dropped it and with his front paws scooped it backward.

The last snake met a similar end. Oberon simply stepped on it with his massive front paw. He held it there, staring down, until Byron came over and picked it up. With a quick twist of his hand, it was done.

I wanted to shout. I did shout. "Is that all you got!" I yelled out across the field at Aayma. Before the words finished coming out of my mouth, I regretted them.

CHAPTER 47

WHAT IT WAS

ACROSS THE WAY THE HYENAS WERE ON THE MOVE. They looked like a swarm. The sneaky snake attack was a distraction for this more serious ploy. The snakes were dispatched without difficulty, but to Aayma the distraction was worth it. That didn't work out so well for the snakes, which made me wonder why anyone would follow her. She obviously cared very little for life, and yet there they were, doing what she wanted. Life on our side of the field was spent, too, but on our side it was given. On Aayma's side it was taken.

Byron and his guys stripped down and took on their wolverine forms. The wolves on either side of the center group squeezed in from either side. There was going to be a bull rush aimed at the middle of our defense. The pack settled in close, forming a wall in preparation for the impact that was rushing headlong up the hill toward them with reckless abandon.

I found myself squinting the way I would have squinted just before the impact of a car crash I could see coming. I also held the railing in a death grip. Every muscle in my body was preparing for the impact I was about to witness.

That's when it happened. There was no discernable sound, yet it was the loudest thing I had ever heard. It was so loud I could literally feel my eardrums flex inward. I wasn't touched either, but it knocked me back across the deck and against the opposite railing. What was affecting me so strongly wasn't a sound or a touch. It was a bright light, so bright it should have blinded me. It didn't blind me, but it did knock me over and clog my ears.

Other than when I was flying backward, I saw everything. It was an explosion of blinding bright light that appeared suddenly in the middle of what was a skirmish in the moments before impact. The explosion didn't fall from the sky or rise up from the earth. One moment nothing was there, and the next a dot of light appeared in their midst. Then it grew so rapidly and so forcefully that everything around it was thrown back away from it.

The wave of light knocked everything—not just me, but everything else, even the massive Oberon—off their feet. Everyone had to scramble back into balance. For me that just meant getting back to the rail so that I could see what was happening. For Aiden and the pack it meant getting back on all fours to be ready for the hyenas, who were surely getting themselves ready to charge again.

The light, whatever it was, didn't recede, but it did dim down to a dull glow. Standing in the middle of the dull glow were three radiant men. They were so radiant that I couldn't actually tell if they were men or women. I just assumed they were male. Angels are male, right?

"Get on with it!" screamed Aayma from beyond the light.

The hyenas, which had been milling silently and pacing in front of the angels, began their charge again with the high-pitched yelping that passed for their barks. They lurched forward in unison. Just as quickly as they charged, they froze where they were, because the angel closest to them turned and simply held up his hands.

Seriously, all he did was hold up his hands, and those hyenas stopped where they were. They kept yelping and they kept lurching forward, but it was like they kept hitting an invisible wall. The angel's hands were open, with his fingers spread wide apart. He slowly closed his right hand into a fist, and as he closed his hand the yelping got quieter and quieter, until it was gone altogether. When I say the yelping was gone, I mean the sound was gone. As near as I could tell from where I watched, the hyenas were still yelping with their mouths. There was just no sound.

Aiden and the pack squared up their ranks, but the angel nearest them turned toward them and held his hands out, too. His hands were held out palms down, and he slowly pumped them up and down a few times. When the pack was all seated, he stopped pumping.

The third angel, the one in the middle, spoke first to the angel holding the hyenas back, and then to the angel in front of the pack. Then the third angel walked slowly through the pack and across the compound, glowing all the way.

I watched every step he took until it dawned on me. *He's heading into my house.*

CHAPTER 48

"IT'S TIME"

I WAS DOWN THE STAIRS A SECOND LATER, heading straight for Mom's room.

"You can't have her!" I declared, bursting through the door.

The only two people in the room were Mom, who was still in bed, and Wally, who was sitting next to her with his back to the door I had just come through.

"What's going on, Jasper?" asked Wally, straining his neck around to see me.

"Ahhhh," was my answer. And then another thought came to me. "Carol?" I pointed at him and repeated, "Carol? Where's Carol?"

"She went to the kitchen," answered Wally. "Who can't have who, Jasper?" Wally asked me as I hurried to the kitchen.

I half expected a glow to be coming from the kitchen as I headed down the hallway, but there was no glow. I fully expected that there'd be an angel in the kitchen arguing with Carol, who, like me, would be saying, "You can't take her."

There was no argument either. Instead, there was a polite conversation between Carol and a man. The man was standing with his back to me, so I couldn't see his face, but from the back he just looked like a regular old man. No glow. No radiance. No fire.

Standing in the doorway I waited to consider my options, but none came to my mind. Then the man turned to face me.

"Jasper," said the man. "I wondered when you were going to join us."

I swallowed hard. "Mr. Gabriel?" I asked weakly. I knew it was him, but I didn't believe it was possible either. Mr. Gabriel, the new guidance counselor at the high school, was here in my kitchen talking to my sister, and he got here through an exploding dot of light.

"Yes, Jasper, it's me," he told me. "Don't be afraid." I didn't know it then, but as it turns out, that's his line. He has to say that pretty much wherever he goes.

He gestured to the table. "How about we all sit down for a bit?"

As we sat down, Carol looked at me and asked, "Do you know him?"

Mr. Gabriel and I looked at each other. I sort of hoped he'd answer her question, but he looked at me like he was curious to hear how I would answer her question.

"Mr. Gabriel is my counselor from school," I told her. Looking from her to him, I added, "But I think he's an angel, too." I leaned toward him, trying to coax a confirmation from him, but he turned to Carol.

"*Are* you an angel?" asked Carol more forcefully.

"If you wish," he said unconvincingly. "I'd call myself a messenger if I was going to say something about what I am." To me he added, "Who I am is simply Gabriel."

" 'Gabriel,' " I repeated. "Not 'Mr. Gabriel'?"

"No, not 'Mr. Gabriel.'"

"Did you come for our mother?" Carol asked harshly.

He chuckled. "I am not the angel of death. Do I really look like I could be the angel of death?"

"How would we know?" answered Carol.

He smiled patiently. "Yes, of course. I apologize. I was attempting to be amusing." Clearing his throat he said, "I am not here to bring death. I have come with a message."

"For our mother?" Carol asked.

"No, Carol. I am here for you."

"Me?" she asked, standing up quickly.

He put his hands up and motioned for her to sit back down. When she was seated again, he said, "Many things are out of balance right now. Surely you have noticed this."

Carol nodded yes.

Neither of them paid attention to me, which was fine with me.

"Do you know why there is such imbalance right now?" he asked.

"Because Mom is sick. Everything is out of balance because Mother Nature is sick."

Gabriel nodded in agreement. "That is a very reasonable thought, Carol. If Mother Nature is impaired, it will create an imbalance. But it is true the other way as well."

"What other way?" asked Carol.

"If the imbalance in the world is serious enough, that will make Mother Nature sick. She is tied to the earth the way. . . ." He stopped and looked around the room, searching for how to say what he wanted to say. "We are all creatures, even your mother, Mother Nature. We were created with a purpose in mind. We were also given freedom, but if we use our freedom to turn away from that purpose"—he paused again and leaned toward Carol—"Well, there would be consequences to that. It'd be like a tiger shark trying to live in a tree."

"My mother is sick because she got bit by a black mamba," I stated.

"It's true. She did suffer a black mamba bite, but the venom would not have had an effect on her if"—he paused, looking hard at Carol—"if there had been more balance around her."

"Oh, that's rich," snarled Carol. "You're blaming me." She stood up again and, placing both hands flat on the table, leaned toward Gabriel. "I didn't do anything."

"That is true. You did nothing wrong."

Carol pointed toward the back pasture. "Why aren't you talking to her?"

"I don't have a message for Aayma."

Carol made a fist, but she didn't pound it on the table. "Why not? She's the one who's doing this. If you want to know who's upsetting the balance, it's her."

"That's true," said Gabriel, nodding again. "Aayma wants more than she has been given."

Sitting back down, Carol clamped her jaw and nodded her head once. "That's right. That witch has been given a—a—" Looking at me she asked, "What's that word you kept talking about? You know, yours is with the wolves."

"Dominion," I answered.

"Responsibility," Gabriel corrected me. "When the Creator gives you a dominion, it is not yours to own. It is yours to be responsible for."

"Yes," said Carol. "That witch cares nothing for her dominion. All she wants is more."

"Yes," said Gabriel.

Waving a finger at Gabriel, Carol said, "Good. You agree. So why are you here? Why don't you go across that field and do what it takes to shut her down? You said it yourself. She is trying to take more dominion than she was given."

Gabriel stood up very slowly. After a nod to me he walked to the back door and turned back to Carol. "You are right. The balance is threatened when the Father's servants take more dominion than they are given. Do you know what is in many ways an equal threat to the balance of nature?"

Neither of us answered, but I think Carol knew what he was going to say.

"Taking more is a problem, Carol, but so is taking less." With that he opened the door. Although it was still the middle of the night, light flooded into the room when he opened the door.

"Wait," I urged. "What's the message?"

He smiled at Carol. It was a warm smile. "It is time for you to be you."

"What does that mean?" I asked. I was a little surprised that it was me asking the questions and not Carol.

"She knows what she needs to know," answered Gabriel. "And when she needs to know more, she will." To Carol he bowed and added, "You can't know more, though, until you believe what you already know."

CHAPTER 49

THEY ARE COMING

WE BOTH STARED AT THE DOOR for several seconds after Gabriel had shut it and gone. It was like time had stopped and waited for me. It was a moment of time I didn't know how to leave. Finally I realized that something worth watching might be going on outside.

"Come on," I urged Carol just before heading back up the stairs to the observation deck on the roof.

Carol was still in a sort of trance, staring at where Gabriel had been. When I spoke to her, she stood up slowly and looked at me, but I'm not sure if she was seeing me yet. I was sure about the fact that she wouldn't be following me. What Gabriel expected her to do was beyond me, but I was equally sure she wouldn't be following him either.

I got to where I could see the pasture just as Gabriel made his way through the pack. He was glowing again. He returned to what I assume was his spot in the middle. Once he was standing still, the other two backed toward him until they were standing right next to each other. The one facing the pack was still holding his hands out palms down, but as soon as he was right next to Gabriel, he turned them palms up and slowly raised them. As he did this, the pack rose up off their hindquarters and got into defensive positions.

The angel facing the hyenas was still holding up his hands. His left hand was open, and his right still closed tight into a fist. He opened his fist, and as it opened, the sound of yelping returned. His hands stayed up, and as I knew they would, they held the hyena cackle at bay.

I kept watching because I didn't want to miss what happened to the hyenas. I tried to guess what was going to happen next. Were the hyenas going to burst into flames? Were they going to go crazy and drown themselves, or better yet, turn on Aayma? I was positive that it would be something. After all, we were the good guys, and they were the bad. The angels had to be on our side. They had to be.

Then Gabriel looked up at me and nodded. I was sure it was him saying, "Watch this," to me, but I was wrong. That's when they left. The three of them just shrank down to a dot. Then they were gone, and it was dark again.

For a long moment, both sides stared at each other without moving. I think they were all stunned or confused about what had just happened. I think I was still hoping that what I knew was about to happen wouldn't happen.

Then it happened. The oversized white hyena came from the back and bounded through the hyena ranks, charging right at Oberon. It was the first move, the move that started everything else moving.

Oberon stood and roared.

The white hyena lowered his head and drove himself as hard as he could into Oberon's chest.

Oberon stood his ground, and just before the white beast's head made contact, Oberon swatted him down with a massive blow to its back. The white hyena flattened on the ground, but to my amazement he wiggled back up, only to be struck down again.

Oberon's victory was short-lived, however, as the hyenas were just too many and too close. A wave of them hit the pack as Oberon was delivering the death blow to the white one. The wave pushed us back as it hit, and then it enveloped the pack as wave after wave kept coming.

Maire was the first to fall, but Aiden was quickly over her, protecting her. It was a position that neither of them could survive in for long. I knew if I could get Maire to safety, it would protect them both.

As I flew down the stairs Carol appeared at the bottom.

"Where do you think you're going?" she demanded in her motherly voice.

"Out there," I told her as I rushed by.

"Oh, no, you're not," she ordered.

I didn't slow down to debate her.

The field was absolute chaos. Hyenas and wolves were barking, snarling, biting, scratching, and crying out in pain. It is amazing, maybe even a miracle, that amid all that carnage I went untouched. I got to Maire and began to drag her from the field. All around me the battle waged in a frenzied dance as I tried to pull her inch by inch from harm's way.

I got as far as the edge of the action and could go no farther. I was spent and could see no hope. Everywhere I looked, we were losing. We were giving better than we got, but there were just so many of them. Wolves were down and not moving. The wolverines were surviving by their quickness, but they were doing no damage to the enemy. The surviving wolves, one of which was Aiden, had formed a circle for protection, but they were surrounded and overwhelmingly outnumbered. I couldn't see Maggie anywhere. Only Oberon was still holding his own, but he had to be getting tired.

I covered Maire's body as best I could and began to cry. It was all that was left to me. I could hold it back no more.

Then, in my darkest moment—our darkest moment—a single voice rose up above the blare of the battle. It was a woman's voice. "Noooooooo!" she cried.

I looked toward the sound. It was coming from the observation deck, where I had been minutes before. I found her immediately. She was standing there silhouetted by the full moon directly behind her. Both of her fists were raised above her head. Her "no" was haunting in its length and its pitch.

"Mom," I said out loud.

That's when I knew we'd be okay. It was only another few seconds before I found out how. The first one flew right over her head and straight down into the fray. The second and third ones came right after it, and before I knew it there were so many eagles that they blackened even the night sky with their sheer number.

I watched the first eagle swoop down and snatch the hyena that had placed himself directly in front of Aiden. I wouldn't have thought an eagle could pick up something as big as a hyena, but it did. The eagle flew up and across the field. When he was over the spot where Aayma was watching, he dropped his passenger.

I didn't see the second and third eagles pick up their victims, but I saw the victims fall toward Aayma. In no time there were so many hyenas falling out of the sky toward Aayma that she retreated back into the woods.

I got nudged off of Maire from behind. It was Aiden. For us the battle was over. For the hyenas the battle was in high gear. They were running for their lives. A few of them made it to the woods. The rest did not survive.

I stood up, tears streaming down my cheeks, and watched my mother do her magic from the observation deck. I wished everybody I ever knew was standing next to me right then so I could tell them, "That's my mom."

CHAPTER 50

"AND SO YOU DID"

IT'S OVER, IT'S OVER, was the chorus that kept going through my head as I headed into the house. Mom had lowered her arms and disappeared from the roof. The chorus in my head changed as I entered the kitchen. *It's over, and Mom is back.*

I hurried through the kitchen to the hallway. I expected Mom to be standing there waiting for me, but she wasn't. Carol was.

"Where's Mom?" I asked her.

Carol didn't say anything. She pointed to her left in the direction of Mom's room.

"Come on," I told her as I hurried past her.

The door to Mom's room was open. Wally was sitting on the far side of her bed, and Mom was propped up slightly on pillows. Her eyes were open.

She looked at me and smiled. Then she patted the bed next to her.

Wally said, "How about this?" as I sat down next to Mom.

I didn't know what to say. It seemed like it had been forever since I had my mother, and now here she was. Nothing else, as incredible as it all was, was on my mind.

"Am I glad to see you," I declared, throwing my arms around her.

Mom leaned forward to make room for my arms. I heard a little moan escape from her as she leaned forward.

"Be careful, Jasper," warned Wally. "She's still pretty weak."

When I let go of her, she settled back against the pillows. With my thumb I motioned toward the ceiling and said, "I guess that really took it out of you."

"What, honey?" she asked.

"You know. Bringing the eagles," I said. "In another few minutes it would have been too late."

She smiled weakly and shook her head no.

"She hasn't been out of that bed, Jasper," Wally told me.

"Then who—?" I began to ask, but I knew the answer. Turning toward the door I found her. Carol was standing in the doorway. In my hurry to get to Mom I hadn't noticed what she looked like, but I was seeing it now. She was pale and slumped over with exhaustion. Her hair looked like she just stepped out of a wind tunnel.

"Mama," said Carol weakly.

Mom held her hands out and said, "Come here, baby."

I got out of the way.

These are the two strongest people I know, and I had never heard them talk like that to each other.

Carol sat where I had been. She buried her head in Mom's neck and began to sob.

Wally and I looked at each other. He seemed like he was thinking what I was thinking: that we shouldn't be here right now, but we shouldn't move either.

We could barely understand Carol say, "I was so scared, Mama."

"I know," said Mom, stroking her hand on Carol's back.

"I almost got Jasper killed," Carol babbled through her tears.

"You saved him, baby."

Carol sat back away from her and looked down. "You're just saying that."

"I'm not," said Mom. "I watched you. When Jasper went outside, you tried to stop him, and when that didn't work, you went to the roof."

"How?" asked Carol. It was a question I wondered about, too.

"How did I watch you?" smiled Mom. "I saw you through Kitty."

"'Kitty,'" repeated Carol as she looked around the room for our Great Pyrenees.

I looked around for Kitty, too. She was curled up in her bed in the corner of the room. I hadn't known she was out of her coma yet. Apparently Carol didn't know that either. Kitty must have followed Carol to the roof. Carol hadn't noticed her.

Carol looked at me. I was standing behind her, out of the way, while she was crying. She held out her hand. When I took it, she pulled me up alongside her. "Are you okay?"

I nodded yes.

"Are you okay?" Mom asked Carol.

"I don't know," said Carol, glancing at Wally.

Wally smiled tenderly. With his hand he waved Carol back to Mom.

"I'm sorry, baby," said Mom. "I've tried to protect you from this." Mom held her hand out to me. "I tried to protect you both from this." Looking back to Carol she said, "I made some huge mistakes with you, though. I knew your dominion would be eagles, just like Jasper's is wolves. I knew Linus's was attracted to bears, but I didn't trust that until now."

"Linus's dominion is bears?" repeated Carol.

"Well, that explains Oberon," observed Wally.

"When you were little, we took you to an eagle sanctuary. We thought the exposure would help you get used to them. We knew they'd be responsive to you, but there were too many and you were too young. They swarmed all over you, and you got over-whelmed. We've kept it from you ever since. I'm sorry. We thought we had more time."

"That explains your nightmares," said Wally.

"It explains other things, too," added Aunt Maggie from the door. "This isn't the first time you saved Oberon, and it's not the first time you saved your brother either."

Carol pointed at her. "When Mom was saying, 'We,' she meant her and you, didn't she?"

Maggie nodded.

"Carol sent eagles to save me on the road outside of Rich-mond when I—"

"When you disobeyed me," Aunt Maggie finished my sen-tence. "And yes, she did."

"I didn't send the eagles," protested Carol. "I wouldn't know how."

"You did. You may not know how, but you don't know how you make your lips move, either," countered Maggie.

Looking at Mom, Carol asked, "You know how it works, don't you?"

"You willed it. When your brother was in danger, you forgot your fear and asserted your will," explained Mom.

"It's really that simple?" asked Carol.

"Yes, if it is truly yours to do. Otherwise, no," answered Mom.

To me, Carol said, "That sounds like Gabriel."

"Gabriel," chuckled Mom. "Was he here?"

"He came to talk to Carol," I answered.

"What did he have to say, Carol?"

"He said I'd know when I know."

"And so you did."

CHAPTER 51

DOING WHAT COMES NATURALLY

IT WAS OVER, AND WE ALL RETURNED to normal and lived happily ever after. No? I didn't expect anyone would believe that anymore than I do. It was over, though. At least that chapter in our lives was over. Mom was well on her way to being her old self, and the rest of us were getting ready to understand what Mom being her old self meant.

Aunt Maggie went back to being her old self immediately, with one fairly unsettling difference. Maggie was no longer the designated breakfast maker. Carol acquired breakfast duty, which freed Maggie to spend her nights outside, where she, as a black panther, could do what comes naturally to black panthers. That was just going to be something we'd have to get used to, although her walking naked through the kitchen during breakfast was going to take me a bit more time.

Wally finished setting up his lab and has contacted the FDA about a black mamba antivenin he's working on. Sometimes he mentions how much marketing people would love to sell an antivenin made from the antibodies of Mother Nature herself. When he told us that at dinner one night, Carol said, "You wouldn't dare." Mom just laughed and told him to go ahead.

Carol and I have never talked about what happened that day. I'm sure we will, but I'll wait for her to start that. I owe her my life. We all do. But saying thanks was going to have to wait until she was ready. We've all noticed that she's spending more and more time on the roof, so something's happening.

Mr. Gabriel wasn't in school that next Monday, and on Tuesday we were told that he had taken a position in Escondido, California. I can't help but wonder what's going on in Escondido, but I doubt the bad thing that could happen will happen now that he's there.

Oberon just disappeared. Once the eagles had cleared the field and won the day, there were still a few hyenas that fled into the woods. Aiden sent the remnant of the pack in after them. Oberon went, too. He just never came back. At first it scared me because Aayma was still around somewhere, and I thought she might have done something to him.

Maggie said, "Not with the Mother awake, she wouldn't."

"That's his way," added Byron. "The big guy isn't so big on hanging around, but he'll be back if y'all need him."

Byron and the wolverines stuck around another week, looking for any signs of black mambas but found none.

"That's one real shy snake," said Byron before they left.

We never found Aayma. That fact was particularly bothersome to Byron and the wolverines. They wanted a different kind of end than we got. Aiden never said, but I'm pretty sure he also wanted a different end than we got. From the beginning Maggie said that destroying Aayma was possible. As for Mom, she just said, "Aayma has her place."

Most of us were sitting around the kitchen table when Mom said that. Byron's response was to ask, "Yeah, but will she stay in her place?"

"It's not in our power to eliminate disease, but we don't have to give it opportunity, either," said Mom.

Aunt Maggie looked up toward the roof when Mom finished speaking. That's when I noticed Carol wasn't at the table.

So, they all left. It was right away with Oberon. A week later it was Byron and the wolverines. Then the Pack began to dwindle. Finally, on the night before the Watauga High School graduation, the only wolves still with us were Aiden and Maire.

I spent the evening with Dirk and Cathy, and Harlan and Evans. We had dinner at Bombadil's. Oberon's oversized table on its own separate platform was gone, which led to wild speculation about where Oberon was. Evans speculated that Oberon was off grooming himself to be a professional wrestler. Harlan, ever the skeptic, was sure that Oberon was doing time for something in his past that had caught up with him. Her argument was that he didn't exist on paper, which to her meant that he wasn't who he said he was. I just listened, but it was fun to think about Evans's theory.

Something was missing from our dinner conversation: Riley. It was me and two couples, and even though I'm part of a couple, too, my other wasn't mentioned. Riley was due to come in for graduation on Saturday. We all knew that, but it was still strange that Riley wasn't mentioned. For my part, I was too busy not saying what I knew about Oberon to notice that no one else was mentioning Riley either. I discovered why no one had mentioned Riley all night when my dessert came.

"Are you going to eat all that by yourself, sir?" asked the waitress from behind me, as she placed the mint brownie covered with mint chocolate chip ice cream and hot fudge in front of me.

"Riley!" I said excitedly. I knocked my chair over when I stood up, but she caught it before it hit the floor. She managed to get the chair righted without dropping the two spoons she brought, but she didn't hang on to them when I lunged at her.

As she picked up the spoons I looked at everyone and announced, "Riley's here."

They laughed at me, but I didn't care. When Riley stood back up, I told her the same thing. We had talked at least twice a day, but she hadn't told me that she would come back early.

We got fresh spoons and made good use of them. I'm sure I was the brunt of several jokes from Evans and Harlan, but I wasn't paying attention. I had just put a spoonful of ice cream in Riley's mouth when her cell phone rang.

With the spoon still in her mouth she looked at her phone and mumbled, "It's 9:30."

"What happens at 9:30?" asked Cathy.

Riley pulled the spoon out of her mouth and licked the fudge from the back before saying, "My dad's picking me up out front then." Turning to me she asked, "Walk me out?"

I don't think I hid my disappointment very well, but I managed to say, "Of course."

Riley took my arm as we walked outside. "Guess what, Jasper?"

"You're moving back to Boone," I guessed, because that's what I wanted. It wasn't really my guess, because just a few days ago when we'd talked about it, she told me her father had gone to look at a business out west.

"We're moving back to Boone," she said, using the very words I had said sarcastically. She didn't giggle, but she had a huge grin and her shoulders were scrunched up.

"What happened? I thought he was dead set against coming back here."

"I don't know what happened, but he went to some kind of business seminar on his trip. All I know is he came home and said he had to be true to his true self, and that meant being in the pharmaceutical business with your brother-in-law. Isn't that great?"

"It is," I told her, but she was disappointed in my lack of enthusiasm. I was excited about her coming home, but I was also intrigued about what happened to her father. Out of curiosity I asked, "Where exactly did your father go?"

"Some town in California called Escondido."

When I got home, Aiden and Maire were waiting for me in the kitchen. It was only 10:30, but no one else was up.

"Hey," I said, scratching Kitty, who had made peace with the wolves.

I was in a great mood. Aayma was gone, school was out for the summer, and Riley would be moving back. But the look Maire gave Aiden wiped that all out. She didn't smile, but smiling wasn't her thing anyway. She looked at Aiden like she knew he was about to do something he dreaded. I knew right away what it was he was about to do. I'm sure I knew that time was coming, but I never allowed myself to think it.

I was standing frozen next to the door as Maire approached me. Our eyes were locked together. She looked sad as she took hold of my face with both her hands and looked deeply into my eyes. She never said anything, but it didn't matter. Still holding my face she leaned back and bowed her head the way a servant would. She didn't look directly at me again. When she let go of my face she glanced at Aiden and then circled around me and out the back door.

Looking at Aiden was the last thing I wanted to do right then. I wasn't prepared. I had plenty of time to prepare, but I didn't think about it. I would have had to admit this moment was coming to be prepared, so I didn't really want to prepare. But now that the moment had come I didn't want to be unprepared either.

"You're leaving," I said. My voice trembled.

"We are," he said, stepping closer. "It is time."

"Does it have to be?" I begged.

He didn't answer.

"I know," I sighed. "Will I see you again?"

"For your sake, I hope not, Jazz-barr. If I am called on again, I will gladly come, but I hope it will not be necessary."

I had to press my lips together hard to be able to keep talking. "I don't know if I can say what I want to say."

"You don't need to say anything to me, Jazz-barr, but I want to thank you for your care for us. I know I barked at you when you left the house to protect Maire, but I admired you for that at the same time. We all admired you for that. It matters to us that we matter to you." He bowed his head the way Maire had. When he looked back up, he said, "We are yours."

I stepped back against the door. I was afraid he'd try to leave the way Maire had left. "I never knew my father, but when I imagine what kind of man he was, I imagine you."

He bowed again. "I'm not a man, Jazz-barr."

"Maybe you aren't, but you're the best man I know." The tears were all over my face. I kept my eyes down as I continued, "When all this was going on, I felt like I had to pretend to be a man, but I'm not a man. I'm a kid pretending to be a man. The only time I didn't feel like I had to think about it was when you were around." I looked up at him and added, "Someday I want to be a man like you."

I knew that was all I was going to be able to say, so I lowered my head and grabbed him around his middle and squeezed. The tears were flowing, but I wasn't sobbing until he squeezed me back. He held me like that until my crying ran out of gas.

"Jasper," whispered my mother right next to me. Her arm was making its way between Aiden and me. She was transferring me from Aiden to herself. "He has to go," she whispered in my ear once she had me.

Aiden put his hand on my back and leaned close enough to my ear that I could feel his breath. "I was always watching. Being a man is doing what is necessary to do. In the pack we call that taking your place. It means accepting your responsibility. And that is what I saw you do. You were not pretending."

⟢

Riley and I attended graduation. The seniors all looked magnificent in their formal attire, but Harlan and Evans were the most stunning. I would have expected Harlan to have spiked her hair or dyed it bright pink, but instead she looked like a prom queen with the way her hair and makeup were done. It was Evans who dyed his hair.

Riley grinned when she saw Evans. Under her breath she said, "That's a nice gesture, but baby blue is the wrong color."

The valedictorian was Keely West, the captain of the girls' soccer team. At one point in her speech she said, "What makes the extraordinary occurrences in our lives possible are the multitude of ordinary events that equip us for those moments, so let us celebrate each in its season. For it is the ordinary that is the backbone of the extraordinary."

Riley leaned against me and whispered, "And you were afraid you were the most ordinary member of your family."

I was.

THE END

ACKNOWLEDGMENTS

Special thanks to:

Jocelynn Gingrich and Hanna Smyth for reading and suggestions

Bob Land (www.PastorsPress.com) for editing

Gary Rosenberg (www.TheBookCouple.com) for composing

DeeDee Galliher for proofreading

Cam Collins and Dyan Buck for help with the cover

Barb Thompson for making my life work

www.ingramcontent.com/pod-product-compliance
Lightning Source LLC
Chambersburg PA
CBHW070612130626
46556CB00001B/339